He missed her. He missed her laugh and her bouncy curls. He missed her perfume and her honey eyes.

The claustrophobic loom of the skyscrapers gave him the creeps, and the coldness of all that glass and concrete made it feel so chilly. He missed the bush. He missed the earthy smell and the wide-open spaces. The perfect blueness of the endless sky. The perfect blackness of the star-sprinkled night.

But mostly he just missed Georgina. He looked at the framed picture of her that Cory had painted, which hung on the lounge room wall, and remembered her asking him what was more important—a thirty-year-old dream or Cory's happiness? And he had told her that as long as they were together Cory would be all right. But his nephew wasn't all right, and he wasn't either.

He looked at her portrait. Luckily he knew how to put it right. After he'd put Cory to bed, he picked up the phone, a big smile on his face.

For the first time in two years things felt right.

BACHELOR DADS
Single Doctor… Single Father!

At work they are skilled medical professionals, but at home, as soon as they walk in the door, these eligible bachelors are on full-time fatherhood duty!

These devoted dads still find room in their lives for love…

It takes very special women to win the hearts of these dedicated doctors, and a very special kind of caring to make these single fathers full-time husbands!

SINGLE DAD, OUTBACK WIFE

BY
AMY ANDREWS

™MILLS & BOON®

Pure reading pleasure

First published in Great Britain 2007
Large Print edition 2008
Harlequin Mills & Boon Limited,
Eton House, 18-24 Paradise Road,
Richmond, Surrey TW9 1SR

ISBN: 978 0 263 19926 0

Set in Times Roman 15¾ on 17¾ pt.
17-0108-60321

Printed and bound in Great Britain
by Antony Rowe Ltd, Chippenham, Wiltshire

As a twelve-year-old, **Amy Andrews** used to sneak off with her mother's romance novels and devour every page. She was the type of kid who daydreamed a lot, and carried a cast of thousands around in her head, and from quite an early age she knew that it was her destiny to write. So, in between her duties as wife and mother, her paid job as Paediatric Intensive Care Nurse and her compulsive habit to volunteer, she did just that! Amy lives in Brisbane's beautiful Samford Valley, with her very wonderful and patient husband, two gorgeous kids, a couple of black Labradors and six chooks.

Recent titles by the same author:

AN UNEXPECTED PROPOSAL
THE SURGEON'S MEANT-TO-BE BRIDE
CARING FOR HIS CHILD
MISSION: MOUNTAIN RESCUE

This book is dedicated to all rural and remote health care workers who do a fantastic job despite being under-funded and under-resourced. Thank you.

CHAPTER ONE

ANDREW MONTGOMERY clutched his seat and shut his eyes tight as the tiny plane hit yet another air pocket. *Great, just great.* He held his breath, the bumpy ride a perfect metaphor for his turbulent life.

The pilot beside him whooped with glee. 'Sorry about that, Doc,' said Bomber.

Andrew opened his eyes and found himself thinking unaccustomed thoughts of murder at five thousand feet. He should have known when the guy in Human Resources Management had said 'mail run' that he was going to be squished into a machine that against the vast endless blue backdrop of the outback sky appeared no bigger than a mosquito. And buzzed like one, too.

'Nearly there, Doc.'

Andrew nodded and breathed deeply for the first time in the two-hour flight. He shifted slightly in the seat, trying to get comfortable. He felt as if his knees were up around his ears in the cramped confines. It was all right for Bomber. He was five two if he was lucky, although quite how he fitted his impressive beer gut behind the controls Andrew wasn't sure. With his beard and ruddy cheeks, Bomber looked like he'd walked off the set of a movie and if he hadn't been flying around in a tin can, Andrew would no doubt have appreciated the authentic outback character.

Bomber banked to the left and Andrew shot a hand up to the ceiling of the plane, not that far above his head and braced himself. *Please, God, just let me get on the ground safely. I have responsibilities now.*

'Look at that view, Doc. Nothing more beautiful anywhere in the world,' Bomber enthused.

Andrew pried his eyelids open and looked out the small grubby window near his elbow. He thought about the view flying into Sydney, dominated by the harbour and the Opera House or flying into Charles de Gaulle, the grey, aged architecture, the Seine, the Arc de Triomphe, the Eiffel Tower. Had Bomber ever even been outside the country?

Although he did have a point. There was a beauty to the vastness. It was kind of wild and untamed. Earthy. Primitive. But beautiful nonetheless. The blue sky, unblemished by a single cloud, stretched on for ever, arcing down in the distance to meet the rich red earth. He felt like he was inside a giant snow dome, minus the snow, and as the plane hit some more turbulence, as if some child were talking great delight in shaking it vigorously.

Vast tracts of water sparkled in the sun in the aftermath of the wet season. There were obvious signs of it slowly retreating and as the plane bumped along Andrew hoped that by the end of his six weeks it would have receded enough to allow him to drive back to civilisation. Hopefully this would be his last experience with Bomber.

It was surprisingly green and Andrew was struck by the bold clash of colours. The red dirt, the blue sky, the yellow sun, the green foliage. He thought how much Ariel would have loved to have painted it. He pictured her splashing her oils around, stopping periodically to tune into the vibrations of the air, sense the primitive beat of the earth and translate it with startling accuracy. His sister's art had been amazingly spiritual.

'There she blows,' said Bomber.

Memories of Ariel scattered. Andrew ignored the heaviness in his chest, rousing himself from his grief as he followed the direction of Bomber's gnarled finger. He could see a landing strip carved from the red earth, tufts of hardy-looking grass creeping up the edges, threatening a take-over. There were also a couple of corrugated-iron structures and a solitary vehicle with a figure sitting on its bonnet. George Lewis, he presumed.

'Civilisation,' Bomber said.

Bomber's idea of civilisation was obviously a little limited. Andrew couldn't see another building anywhere. Another human, for that matter. Two tin sheds and one person did not civilisation make. He felt like he was about to land on another planet. Mars maybe. It was certainly red enough.

'Hold on to your hat, Doc. We're going in.'

Oh, dear God. Andrew shut his eyes and clutched his seat again. He hated landings the most.

Georgina Lewis heard the drone of Bomber's plane long before she could actually see it. Out here, she could hear a kangaroo jumping from a mile away. She swatted away a lazy fly and reclined back against the Land Rover's bonnet. She'd placed an old blanket on it the minute she'd pulled up so the engine heat wouldn't give her third-degree burns and she allowed herself the luxury of indulging in the drugging heat of the morning sun.

She shouldn't. With her red hair and freckles there was a very fine line between pleasure and pain. One minute too long and she'd pay—big time. She'd be as red as a beetroot and peeling for days. Not to mention the freckles. And the melanoma risk.

For the millionth time since puberty she found herself lamenting her skin type. Had it really been fair to bless her with a pear shape but not compensate her somehow? She'd kill for beautiful, unblemished olive skin. Skin that purred in the sun and welcomed the gentle kiss of UV rays like those of a masterful lover. Unlike hers, that punished her regularly for her sun worship with the harsh sting of sunburn and rapid multiplication of big brown freckles.

She sighed and bent her knees up, placing her feet on the solid bullbar, her dusty boots gripping the rusty metal easily. She pushed thoughts of her genetic faults aside. The day was beautiful, she had sunscreen on and there was just something about lying totally alone in the middle of nowhere under an azure sky. She felt at peace. At one with nature. Somehow even wearing clothes seemed an insult in this wide primitive land.

She adjusted her Akubra down over her face, hiding the quick smile. Now, wouldn't that be a surprise for the city doctor? Being greeted by a naked nurse. Of course, Bomber would probably die of a heart attack on the spot as well. His hypertension was uncontrolled and his cholesterol was through the roof and, frankly, he was too valuable to lose. How he maintained his pilot's licence she'd never know.

She turned her head towards the approaching drone and could see the glint of sun on metal in the distance. She sat up and shaded her eyes with a hand as she pushed her hat up on her head. She sighed again. Another city doctor. If someone else had been there, she could have made a bet with them about Andrew Montgomery's attire.

Would he be in Armani, like the last two? Or be fully kitted out in R.M. Williams moleskins and full-length Driza-bone coat like the one before? They either thought they were there to drove cattle or dip sheep or treated everyone like hicks, like something that smelt bad on the bottom of their shoes.

Would anyone *normal* ever get off that plane? Someone who was genuinely interested in the work they did, instead of using the mandatory experience merely as a tick on their CV? Maybe someone who would stay and take the reins from a suddenly aged professor?

Georgina worried her bottom lip as the speck grew bigger. The prof wasn't getting any younger. He seemed a little frailer these days and she couldn't help but wonder if there wasn't something sinister behind it. The man was seventy and for the first time he was looking it. Yes, he was still as sharp as a tack, indisputably ran rings around those snooty city boys, but he was a little slower, a little less nimble.

All the prof wanted now was to bow out. Retire. Buy a tinnie and go fishing. Surely that wasn't too much to ask for a great man who'd spent his life committed to ridding remote Australia of preventable blindness? A doctor who had earned many accolades in a very distinguished career, whose work was respected worldwide and his papers printed in the most prestigious medical journals. But Georgina knew as well as everyone else in these parts Professor Harry James would never just down tools and leave his programme in the lurch.

She pushed herself off the vehicle, landing with practised ease on strong legs. She absently brushed her hands across the fabric covering her much-maligned butt, suddenly nervous as the small plane descended that Andrew Montgomery was going to be another unmitigated disaster. *Just send me someone I can work with.*

Georgina shielded her face as the taxiing plane whipped up clouds of red dust that stung her bare arms. She looked up when the dust settled and saw the prop cut out on the now stationary plane. Bomber waved at her through his grimy windshield and she grinned at him. She could barely make out the passenger's features through the lingering haze and was distracted anyway by Bomber's whoop of joy as he exited the plane.

'George! George!' he called.

Georgina grinned at his enthusiasm and prepared herself for the inevitable energetic greeting. He strode towards her, his long snowy beard, rotund build and bulbous red nose making him perfect for his self-appointed role as Santa. Every Christmas Day he hopped into his little plane and flew from property to property ho-ho-ho-ing all the way, giving out gifts and sweets to all the kids.

He wrapped her up in a big bear hug and, despite being taller than her by just a whisker, lifted her off her feet and spun her around. She laughed and shrieked at him to put her down as dizziness threatened.

'How's my best girl?' he asked, setting her down.

'You've been asking me that since I was five years old, Bomber.' Georgina grinned good-naturedly, waiting for the world to right itself.

Bomber's face broke into an easy grin. 'Did you grow up? I didn't notice,' he said.

Georgina laughed. 'So, what's the verdict?' she asked, gesturing towards the plane with a nod of her head. 'Armani or R. M. Williams?'

'Neither.' Bomber laughed. 'He didn't say much. I think he's got a lot on his mind. But I think this one may be…normal.'

Georgina gasped dramatically and smiled at

Bomber as she looked over his shoulder. 'He's taking a while to get out of the plane. Does he know how? You don't think he expects me to open the door for him, does he?' she asked. A dozen uncharitable thoughts steamed through her head.

Bomber chuckled. 'I think he needs a minute. Don't think he's a flyer.' He winked.

Oh, great. Just what they needed. A city boy with a delicate stomach. 'Excellent,' she sighed.

'I'll get the mail,' Bomber said.

Georgina watched Bomber head back towards the plane and thought mutinous thoughts about Andrew Montgomery. She would not pander to him. She stood staring at the plane, waiting impatiently, her hands on her hips. His door opened a few moments later. *And about time, too.*

Andrew just resisted the urge to sink to his knees and kiss the red dirt. It didn't matter how big the plane was, being on the ground again was always the best part of flying. It felt good to be on *terra firma* and he took a moment to inhale the warm air deep into his lungs. He could smell the dirt and its earthy aroma was just the grounding effect his unsettled stomach needed.

He walked around the back of the plane and joined Bomber at the open hatch to the cargo hold.

'You right, Doc?' Bomber asked.

'Yes thank you, Bomber. I am now.'

The pilot nodded and passed Andrew his backpack. 'Better not keep George waiting,' he said.

Andrew put on his sunglasses as he turned and looked in the direction that Bomber had inclined his head. So this was George Lewis?

'George is a…girl,' Andrew said, mildly surprised that the person he'd been corresponding with was female. *And a very interesting-looking female at that.*

Bomber chuckled. 'That she is. Georgina Lewis.'

Andrew blinked, mildly surprised at the instant flare of attraction. *Goodbye, George, hello, Georgina.* How long had it been since a woman had had such an immediate effect?

He slung his backpack over his shoulder and walked towards his lift, finally enjoying the scenery.

A hint of copper curls the colour and richness of the earth beneath their feet brushed her shoulders, ill disguised by the shadow of the broad-brimmed Akubra. A face full of freckles enhanced her features, rather than detracted from them. She had high cheekbones and a wide mouth with full, soft lips. Her nose was dainty and turned up a little at the end and she had eyes the colour of iron bark honey. His favourite blend.

She was short—he figured he towered a good foot above her. But her wide, assertive stance left him in no doubt that she curved in all the right places. A T-shirt would have normally camouflaged the dip of her waist but thanks to her hands-on-hips stance, it was emphasised beautifully. Her waist was small, her fingers nearly spanning the circumference of it, almost meeting in the middle. And her hips flared out from under her hands, full and luscious.

She wore hipster-style three-quarter-length cargos that finished mid-calf. Durable work boots, hardly the height of fashion, covered her feet, and thick socks that had bunched down around the cuff of her boots allowed a small glimpse of sturdy calf muscles. Her black T-shirt fitted snugly across her impressive chest.

'Georgina?' he asked as he approached.

'George,' she corrected, holding her hand out. 'Dr Montgomery, I presume?' she said.

'You're not what I expected,' he said, taking her hand, surprised by her firm grip and businesslike shake.

Georgina withdrew her hand. Yep, she'd heard that one before. 'I guess that makes us even,' she said.

He raised an eyebrow. She seemed annoyed with him for some reason. Georgina Lewis looked like she didn't suffer fools gladly. Her body may have been round and feminine but that's where it ended. Her whole hands-on-hip demeanour was no nonsense. She looked tough—capable and strong.

Not really his type at all. Although it had been a long time since he'd been interested in a woman, he wasn't sure he knew what his type was any longer. And even if she had been, there was a definite 'back off' aura around her that was coming through loud and clear. 'Well, now, I was expecting a bloke. What were you expecting?'

Nothing like you. How could Bomber have got it so wrong? This man was as far from normal as you could get. OK, he wasn't some pretentious city boy, playing dress-up, but the man was utterly gorgeous. Long-legged, broad-shouldered, flat-stomached. Six plus feet of pure sex appeal. His blond wavy hair sat perfectly, his teeth were white and even, his smile was lazy and his eyes were so blue a person could fall in and drown in them and be dead before they knew what hit them.

He even had a scar. An uneven slash, about five centimetres long and thicker in the middle, drove a white path through the dark stubble of his jaw line. It didn't look like it had been attended to by some posh city surgeon either, just hastily sewn together and left to heal. She found herself wondering how he'd got it and admiring its utter sexiness.

And he was sexy. Simply gorgeous. Joel gorgeous. Oh, he didn't look like her ex remotely, Joel had been dark to this man's fair, but the instant flare of attraction was ringing bells and flashing warning signs. She remembered the havoc Joel had wreaked, how broken her heart had been, and ruthlessly tamped down on the excited flutter. Pretty city boys were not her thing. Not any more. Not ever again.

She shrugged, struggling for nonchalance. She mustn't give this man an inch. 'Am Armani suit. Maybe a Driza-bone.'

He frowned. 'You said jeans and T-shirts, right?'

She nodded her head. But few of the city docs actually took that on board. And it wasn't exactly fair that this man should fill denim and cotton better than any man on earth.

'Here's the mail, George,' Bomber said, interrupting, and she could have kissed him for his timing. 'Some are for Byron and the rest are for the prof. Medical supplies mainly.'

'Thanks Bomber, leave it there. I'll just open the back,' she said, grateful to be moving away from the disturbing Andrew Montgomery.

Andrew took the reasonably heavy box from

Bomber, watching the sway of her hips as he followed her. He smiled to himself at the lushness, the beauty of their roundness and then blinked and shook his head, realising his thoughts were leading him somewhere he didn't want to go. Again he was surprised at his reaction. His grief had left him completely disinterested in the opposite sex and his subsequent responsibilities hadn't left him any time anyway. Maybe the dark veil was finally lifting?

It didn't matter anyway. Relationships were not on the agenda. He was here for six weeks only. It was one of his last mandatory rotations before finally qualifying as a consultant ophthalmologist. And a damn inconvenient one at that. The juggling he'd had to do to get here still had his head spinning. It'd better be worth it.

He sure as hell didn't need a tough-as-nails country lass, even if she was stunning, getting into his head, complicating his already complicated enough life. He joined Georgina at the back of the vehicle and stowed the box.

'I could have managed,' Georgina protested, and he shrugged.

'May as well be useful,' he said, although he didn't doubt her capabilities for a moment.

Five minutes later the supplies were packed and

George had waved goodbye to Bomber. Andrew climbed in, dubious that a vehicle that appeared to be more rust than anything else would actually start, let alone get them to where they needed to go. He slammed the heavy door shut and buckled up, the smell of petrol, grease and rust and something else assaulting his senses. Flowers, he decided.

Georgina joined him and the smell intensified. *Great, she smells like flowers.* He suppressed the urge to move in closer, preferring the smell of her to the more earthy smell of rusty truck.

'Who's Byron?' he asked.

'This is,' she said, gesturing to the vista before them. 'Byron Downs.'

She started the car and much to his surprise it roared instantly to life. A rock song blared out at him on a blast of hot air from the vents and between the noise of it and the engine he couldn't hear himself think.

Georgina reached for the volume dial and turned it down quickly. But not off. 'Sorry,' she apologised. 'There's only one way to listen to rock music as far as I'm concerned—full bore. Although I do appreciate that not everyone sees it that way.'

'Rock chick, huh?' he said, when he could hear himself speak.

'To the end.' She nodded vehemently.

The passion in her eyes turned them to a particularly attractive shade of liquid gold. 'Thought it was country music out here?'

'Now, there's a stereotype I haven't heard before,' she said sarcastically, shifting gears emphatically.

Andrew chuckled. *Prickly!* He looked hastily out of the window as the rutted ground they drove on sent vibrations through the entire car that wobbled interestingly through her chest. He searched for a safe topic of conversation.

'I saw this band at Wembley years ago,' he said. It seemed like a million years ago now as he reached back beyond his grief to capture the memory.

Georgina brought the car to an abrupt halt, almost catapulting Andrew into the windscreen. Lucky for him he'd buckled up. 'No way!' she said.

Andrew pushed his face away from the close proximity of the dashboard. 'No. Really. I did. I was nineteen. They were amazing.'

Georgina stared at Andrew Montgomery's beautiful face with the mysterious scar and tried not to imagine how hot he must have looked at nineteen. At a rock concert. Instead, she put the car in gear and got under way again.

Andrew bumped and swayed with the roll and

shudder of the ancient four-wheel-drive. They seemed to be going cross-country at the moment and he hoped Georgina knew where she was going because there didn't appear to be any track and certainly no sign of anything in the distance worth heading to. His window was much cleaner than the one on the plane had been and the scenery was really very beautiful.

It was flat, stretching into the distance. A unique and wild land. Scrubby on the whole but the foliage was lush, not drying and dead, and there were large patches of pink and yellow wildflowers. Its vastness was overwhelming, perversely claustrophobic in its span. If he were agoraphobic, he'd be breathing into a bag by now.

'So who owns Byron Downs?' he asked.

'My family does.'

Ah. That explained how she seemed to know where she was going when there didn't appear to be anywhere to go. 'How many acres is it?'

'Two hundred thousand,' she said.

He whistled. 'Landed gentry, huh?'

'Hardly,' she snorted.

Andrew looked back out the window. Of course, he should have known that Georgina belonged here. It was in every nuance and movement of her body. The way her feet had straddled the ground back at the strip, subconsciously claiming owner-ship. Like she'd played in the dirt as a child, swum in the billabongs, camped out under the stars. She seemed at ease, at one with the world. Very few people he'd ever met had that quality about them.

God knew, he didn't. Not these days anyway. In fact, not for a long time. The realisation a couple of years ago that ophthalmology wasn't his thing had taken him by surprise. He'd fought it, sure, un-willing to abandon the reasons he'd gone into it in the first place. But the restlessness had gone from a gentle nag to a loud resentful bellow deep inside. And just as he had finally realised he had to be true to himself, Ariel had died and had sealed his fate, trapping him there for ever.

His thoughts drifted as he watched the scenery go by. Everything was so vast out here. Even after half an hour he felt as insignificant as a speck of sand in the middle of space. His problems seemed less weighty, too. The beauty, the sheer enormity of the land was strangely soothing to his seething mind and his aching soul.

He sat up straighter and dismissed the fanciful thoughts immediately. He'd been in the outback for less than an hour. He'd grappled with his career quandary for two years. And his beloved twin sister was dead, tragically killed in her prime. He refused to think that this ancient land had already given him a degree of inner peace that he hadn't been able to find at home.

'So, where are we headed?' he asked in an effort to derail his thoughts.

'We're going to the homestead to drop the mail off first.'

'How long will that take?' Andrew asked, peering out the windscreen for some sign of a dwelling.

'An hour,' she said. 'Then we'll head out to the base.'

Andrew opened his mouth to speak again.

'Another hour,' she said, pre-empting his question.

'That's where Professor James is?' he asked.

Georgina nodded. 'The team moved to the new base this morning while I came and picked you up.'

'How long do you usually spend at each base?'

'Normally only two or three days. Depends on how many ops we need to perform. But a lot of the communities are only just accessible again after the wet season so we'll need to spend a little longer.'

Her favourite song from the album began and Georgina reached out for the volume button through pure habit. She pulled herself up short.

Damn! A good blast of rock would be just the distraction she needed from his denim-clad thigh in the periphery of her vision. It may be covered but the jeans moulded his quads well and she just knew his leg would be magnificent underneath.

'It's OK.' He grinned and spun the volume dial up for her. The song was a masterpiece and deserved to be belted out.

Georgina relaxed and smiled at him gratefully. Then wished she hadn't. He smiled back, emphasising his scar, and the impact on her equilibrium was disastrous. If they'd been on a road, she'd have probably run them straight off. She hastily brought her eyes back to the task at hand.

But not before she also recognised a slight flicker of pain in those blue, blue depths. The way his smile, although instantly ramping up his attractiveness, wasn't quite fully reflected in his gaze. Her hands gripped the wheel. She recognised that look. God knew, she'd seen it often enough in her own reflection.

Andrew turned back to the window a little surprised at the effect of George's smile. She'd taken her hat off in the car and the copper curls framed her face and the smile glowed in her eyes and her cheeks and softened her cute pink mouth. She didn't wear any make-up. He didn't know any woman who didn't wear make-up. Hell, even Ariel had managed lipstick.

Thankfully, this song was one of the longest in rock history. Andrew needed a while to erase her smile from his brain. For someone who wasn't his type, she was having a disturbing effect on him. He looked out the window, deliberately studying the scenery, the endless flatness like some bizarre moonscape, and tried to ignore how she sung along tunelessly to the chorus.

The song finished and in his peripheral vision he saw Georgina's hand reach to turn the volume down. Andrew didn't look away from the window, discouraging conversation, and was grateful that Georgina wasn't the chatty type.

Soon he started to see cattle. Brahmans. They were feeding on the fertile grass around some sort of creek.

'Is Byron Downs a cattle property?' he asked.

She nodded. 'We have about forty thousand head.'

'Are they bred for export?'

'Most. Some go to the local markets. And we have a couple of thousand stud cattle.'

He whistled again. 'Do you help with the farm stuff?'

'Of course,' she said coolly. 'When I can, in

between my work with the prof. I can muster with the best of them.'

He nodded and looked back to the window. *Of course.* No wonder she seemed so tough—farm life *was* tough. He tried to think of some of the women he knew in Sydney out here, mucking in with the boys, and couldn't picture it.

They drove in relative silence the rest of the way, a steady rock beat serenading them in the background. They eventually got onto a dirt road and came across their first gate. Georgina unbuckled her seat belt and opened her door.

'I'll do it,' Andrew said, placing a stilling hand over hers.

'There's no need,' she said, withdrawing her hand quickly from the warm temptation of his. 'The latches can be tricky and I'm used to doing it.'

'Thanks,' he said, getting out of the car. 'I'm sure I can figure it out.'

Georgina stared after him. She always got the gates. Unless her brother or father were with her but, then, they were used to this work and this land and knew each gate and latch and their idiosyncrasies intimately. None of the city doctors she'd driven in this vehicle had ever offered to help out. Even Joel had happily watched her traipse backwards and forwards a dozen times.

Andrew fumbled a bit but managed and pushed the gate open. He waited for George to drive through before he shut it again and climbed back in the vehicle.

'Thanks,' she said, still surprised by his actions. Maybe Bomber was right? Maybe this one was normal?

The homestead eventually came into view and Andrew observed it as it grew larger. It looked like an oasis and he was surprised by the number of buildings sprawled around the main house.

'It's big,' he said. Just like everything else around there.

Georgina nodded. 'We have ten full-time jackaroos who we accommodate in a bunkhouse and there's several married dongas. There's a few different storage and machinery sheds. Stables. Helipad.'

He blinked. 'Byron has a helicopter?'

She nodded. 'For mustering.'

But of course. She was looking at him like owning a helicopter was the most natural thing in the whole world. Like everyone owned one.

'The homestead is the original one built back in the late 1800s and has been added to over the years. It can sleep up to twenty.'

Andrew looked at the wide verandah of the elegant homestead set on low stumps. It looked graceful. Old. And cool on this day where the sun had developed real bite. French doors opened up onto the verandah along its generous length.

'Nice,' he said appreciatively.

'Thank you. I think so,' she said, braking in front of the house. 'There's John.' She grinned and turned to him. 'Come and meet my brother.'

Andrew stayed in the car for a moment and observed her give her brother a big hug, their affection obvious. If she hadn't have said so, he would have guessed their relationship immediately. Her brother had the same red hair and freckles. Then another man joined her. He was older, with the same red hair and freckles, although shot with varying shades of grey. He, too, swept Georgina into a huge hug.

A boy, about the same age as his Cory, joined them, and Georgina embraced him, enthusiastically sweeping him into the huddle. Andrew observed the close-knit family and envied them their intimacy. So this was what a family looked like. He felt a pang of jealousy at their obvious mutual adoration and unity.

His guilt over leaving Cory behind intensified and warred with the heavy sense of responsibility he'd felt since becoming his nephew's legal guardian. He'd never felt so far out of his depth as he had the last six months. But he was doing this outback stint for Cory, even if his nephew didn't understand the sacrifice.

Georgina hadn't seen her family for a few weeks and it felt good to be back amongst kin.

'Should have known you'd be here. You always could smell Mabel's cooking,' said John.

'Mabel's cooked lamb,' Charlie, her eight-year-old nephew, said enthusiastically.

Mabel had been around since before Georgina's birth. She'd been married to one of their best jackeroos until he'd been killed over two decades ago in a tragic accident. She'd been keeping house for them ever since.

'Hmm, yummy, my favourite.' Georgina laughed, dropping a kiss on Charlie's strawberry blonde hair, keeping her nephew tucked in close.

'That the city slicker?' Edmund Lewis said quietly in his daughter's ear, nodding to the vehicle where Andrew still sat.

'Uh-huh,' she said, still hugging Charlie.

Her brother whistled quietly. 'He's a bit of a looker, sis. Reminds me of—'

'Don't even say it,' Georgina cut him off quickly.

John chuckled. 'Joel,' he said, and accepted his sister's punch on the arm good-naturedly.

Georgina gave her brother a withering look as she squeezed Charlie even closer to remind herself why another Joel would be a very bad idea. She turned and crooked her finger at the city doctor indicating for him to follow.

Andrew unbuckled slowly. Could he sit and watch these people play happy families when he was making such a dismal failure of his?

CHAPTER TWO

MUCH to Andrew's surprise, he enjoyed lunch. A scrumptious meal and pleasant company kept his mind off his own problems.

'Byron Downs,' he said, kick-starting the conversation once they got under way again. 'What's the history behind the name?'

'My great-great grandfather, Sir George Lewis, named the property after Lord Byron,' Georgina said.

'The poet? "She walks in beauty like the night"? That Byron?'

'Yes,' Georgina said, 'that Byron.' She refused to give the flutter in her stomach any credence. So, he could quote Byron. Anyone who'd done grade-eight English could quote that line. Joel had dazzled her with it, too. The real test was, did he know it all? And that was something she didn't plan on finding out. 'Old George was a bit of a romantic, I feel.'

Andrew smiled. 'You weren't named after him, then?' he asked.

'No, I was named after my very practical great-aunt on my mother's side. But the irony of my nickname is not lost on me.'

'So you're not into flowery romantic prose, like old George?'

Georgina looked at him sharply. *Don't even think about it, buddy. I learn lessons well.* 'Not remotely,' she lied.

'Pity. I'm quite a fan of the romantic poets. We could have whiled away the evenings with poetry recitals.'

She looked at him startled and then saw his teasing grin. Her breath struck in her throat, he looked so boyishly charming. She hardened her heart. If he thought he could play suave city boy to her country hick then he could think again. *Been there, done that.* 'Well, then, Bomber's your man, in that case.'

'Bomber?' he asked, astonished. 'Bomber's into romantic poetry?'

Georgina giggled, despite her earlier chagrin. 'Don't judge a book by its cover. Many years ago he was a high-school English teacher.'

'Bomber?'

Georgina nodded and then laughed again at the look of frank incredulity on Andrew's face.

'I assume that's not his real name?' he asked.

'No. It's not. He was a cropduster for many years

in Queensland. Locals said he'd get low enough to almost touch the crops. He looked like he was dive-bombing them like some kind of kamikaze pilot. No one's called him by his real name for forty years. In fact, I don't even know what it is.'

Andrew resumed his scenery-watching. It really was very beautiful and he realised to his surprise that he was having a good time. His stomach was full and he was sitting next to a pretty girl who smelt like a flower garden.

He'd not been able to resist teasing her about the poetry after he'd heard her dismissive tone, as if being romantic was a mortal sin. Tough, capable women obviously didn't need romance. Something about her back-off look had brought out the devil in him, and the old Andrew, who had always enjoyed a spot of banter and a harmless flirt, had emerged. And it had felt good to have him back.

He realised he hadn't expected to enjoy himself. A couple of years ago when his job dissatisfaction had begun, he had looked forward to this distant part of his rotation eagerly. The opportunity to work with Professor James, Australia's most eminent ophthalmologist, was a golden opportunity. But two years down the track, the timing had really sucked.

Ariel had only been gone for six months and

having his eight-year-old nephew come and live with him had been a huge adjustment. And one he was failing at badly. Cory was still so withdrawn, so grief-stricken, and Andrew didn't know how to reach him, especially with his own feelings still so raw.

Having to leave Cory at this point was the last thing the kid needed. But it was a mandatory rotation and after several postponements due to his bereavement circumstances, he hadn't been able to put it off any longer. Historically medical beaurocracy weren't very tolerant with family issues and their patience had worn thin.

And he needed to complete all his rotations as well as pass his final exams if he wanted to become an ophthalmologist. Which, of course, he didn't, but he owed it to Ariel, even more so since her death, and he certainly owed it to Cory to persevere.

He had a child to take care of now. He wanted Cory to go to the most exclusive schools and the best university and have a new car when he got his driver's licence and braces if he needed them and anything else he desired. And that took money. So he didn't have time to change careers. He was stuck on this path, whether he liked it or not.

So with all this going on in the background and having to arrange someone to care for Cory for six weeks and his nephew's betrayed silence as he had left yesterday still fresh in his mind, he really hadn't expected to feel anticipation. He had thought it would be interesting and fascinating and he would learn a lot.

But that it would help ease the guilt a little over his lame 'I'm doing this for you, Cory' statement yesterday—that he hadn't expected.

In half a day he'd met more interesting people than he usually met in one week in Sydney. And they were as large and as colourful as the vast outback canvas. Georgina's brother and father were great blokes. Laid-back, salt-of-the-earth types. Their calloused hands and wiry muscular frames hinted at their tough manual jobs, but their easy laughter and their teasing banter with Georgina and Charlie showed a gentler, caring side.

'How old is Charlie?' Andrew asked.

'Eight.'

Same age as Cory, just as Andrew had suspected. But the difference between Charlie and Cory was amazing. Charlie was happy and garrulous and obviously well adjusted, compared to Cory's monosyllabic, withdrawn personality. Sure, he'd always been a little on the serious side, due to his mother's disability, but it hadn't stopped him from being a bright, happy little boy. Quick with a smile and very, very affectionate. How did he get that Cory back?

'Where's Charlie's mother?' he asked.

'She died,' Georgina said. She heard Andrew's quick indrawn breath and glanced at him. She saw the shock in his gaze and also the sadness there again.

But Charlie seemed so happy. 'How awful,' he said.

Georgina nodded. 'Yes, it was terrible. We had a couple of shocking years at Byron a while back,' she said, remembering the dreadful cascade of events. Her sister-in-law's death and then her mother's, followed closely by Joel's betrayal and finally her very personal but very devastating miscarriage.

Andrew saw a brief glimpse of grief reflected in her gaze. She had been through a hard time, too. They stared at each other for a few seconds in a strange kind of solidarity.

She broke their connection, disturbed by the rawness of emotion she glimpsed in his eyes. 'Charlie was only one—he doesn't remember her.'

Ah. That explained why Charlie seemed OK. 'What happened?' he asked.

'Jen was a vet, she serviced a huge area and had her own plane. It went down in bad weather.'

'That must have been awful for all of you.'

Georgina nodded, feeling touched by the startling sincerity of his tone. 'John was devastated. We all were.'

'I'm sorry.' What else could he say? Losing someone close was a gutting experience and people's trite words, although well meant, were often not helpful.

Georgina appeared to be concentrating on driving and he turned back to the window, his own loss magnified by hers. And now there was nothing to do other than sit and reflect on it. Since his twin sister's death and having taken on Cory, he'd had little time to dwell on his personal loss, and shoving the pain aside had been easier than confronting it. And now was not the time either.

The drive was getting prettier the further they travelled, and he was grateful for the distraction. It was bushier, with lots of long grass and stands of gum trees. They were on a bigger road now, still dirt, but it appeared well kept and looked like it had been recently graded. They had to traverse a few creeks that hadn't yet receded from the road but the Land Rover handled them as if they were mere puddles.

'So, you want to be an eye doctor,' Georgina said after a prolonged silence, feeling she should lighten the mood and attempt some conversation with the man she was going to be working with for the next six weeks, even if he had had such a disturbing effect on such short acquaintance.

Andrew laughed, feeling like his first-grade teacher was patronising him. But he didn't mind. At least it gave him something else to focus on.

Did he? *Yes. No.* 'Yes.'

Georgina noted his slight hesitation. 'Really?'

'Yes,' he said, more emphatically.

'Why?'

'Why not?' He shrugged.

Because you're the most beautiful man I've ever seen, and in my experience men like you become plastic surgeons, or some sort of hot-shot surgeon anyway. Like Joel. 'It doesn't seem very glamorous,' she said.

'Now who's judging a book by its cover?' he teased. He absently rubbed his thumb over the scar on his jaw. 'No. I suppose it's not, compared to some specialties. But I was five when I made up my mind. I've never wanted to be anything else.' *Until recently.*

'Really? That's strange. Most kids want to be firemen or policemen. Hell, I wanted to be Barbie.'

He laughed. 'How'd that work out?'

Georgina looked down disparagingly at her non-Barbie body and sighed. 'Not so good.'

He chuckled and willed himself not to drop his gaze from her face. 'Barbie is overrated,' he said.

Georgina quashed another flutter. His grin, the husky quality of his laugh was really very sexy. He looked less sad now and she preferred this lightness to his vulnerability. Sexy she could cope with, deeply wounded appealed to feminine instincts she didn't want to admit even existed.

'Absolutely. It was a short-lived phase. John got a GI Joe for Christmas one year and I much preferred him,' she said.

But of course. He laughed again and thought how much Ariel would have liked Georgina. He sobered a little, his thumb finding the scar again. 'Actually, it's because of my sister, Ariel. She's blind.'

Was blind. Was. He still wasn't used to referring to her in the past tense. His sister…dead. He still found it hard to come to terms with.

Georgina didn't know what she'd been expecting, but it certainly hadn't been that. 'Oh, Andrew, how terrible,' she said, feeling instantly contrite over her judgment of him as a carefree, glamorous city boy. 'Did she have an accident when you were five?' she asked. He was rubbing at that intriguing scar again. Did that have something to do with it? She was starting to put two and two together.

'No, she was blind pretty much since birth,' he said.

On, no. How terrible, Georgina thought, still not

picking up on the past tense in her compassion for Andrew's sister. 'What happened? Tumour? Maternal infection?'

'No.' He shook his head and looked out the window. Did he really want to talk about this with a complete stranger when even thinking about it stirred all the old feelings of guilt? 'She was my twin. We were born prem at thirty weeks. Ariel developed ROP. And thirty-five years ago, there was no such thing as laser therapy,' he said, keeping it brief.

Retinopathy of prematurity. Although it wasn't something they saw in the bush, Georgina knew it was an abnormality in the way the blood vessels of the retina grew in premi babies. Georgina glanced quickly at Andrew. He wasn't facing her but his body was tense and his voice hinted at deep-seated emotions. 'Is she totally blind?'

He knew he should correct her but it was nice indulging in the fantasy that Ariel, his twin, his soul mate, was still with them. 'No. Not totally. As good as, though. She was legally blind. She could see some colour and light, shapes but not detail. She had about ten per cent vision.'

Georgina suddenly realised they were talking in the past tense. She felt the skin at her neck prickle in warning. 'Could? Had?'

'Ariel died six months ago.'

Georgina heard her breath hiss out as his quiet statement filled the space between them. She could hear the husky note to his voice and knew it must still hurt like hell to say the words. The sadness in his eyes suddenly made sense.

'I'm sorry,' she said. Because she was. Sorry that Ariel's years on earth had been blighted by blindness because she'd seen more than her fair share of blindness out here and knew how heart-breaking it could be, but sorrier still that Ariel's life had been cut short. Like Jen's. Like her mother's. Like her own unborn baby's.

He looked away from the window and nodded acknowledging her sentiment.

'What happened?' she asked.

'It was just a tragic accident. She was struck down on a pedestrian crossing by a car. The woman driving had a seizure at the wheel and lost control of the vehicle.'

'I didn't think people with epilepsy were allowed to drive?'

'They're not. It was her first-ever seizure. She went on to crash into another car and ended up with severe injuries. She spent several weeks in Intensive Care.'

'Was she charged?'

He shrugged. 'What's the point? It was just one of those tragic accidents. And she's a complete cot case over it. Killing Ariel has left her emotionally and mentally traumatised. I feel sorry for her, actually. I doubt she'll ever drive again.'

Georgina was surprised by his compassion for the woman who had struck down his sister. Many wouldn't have been so forgiving. She glanced at his profile, his brow furrowed by a grim expression. Talking about his sister was obviously taking a lot out of him. She felt absurdly like touching him, covering his hand with hers. Her grief may have been six years ago but there were moments when it was still so raw it took her breath away.

Georgina let a few minutes elapse before she changed the subject. 'So let me guess. You plan to specialise in ROP.'

Andrew smiled and turned to face her. 'Good guess. I've been doing largely that for a while now,' he said. 'I've had several offers from different private practices in Sydney.' It was amazing how calm he sounded. How rational. Not a hint of the turmoil his career dilemma had thrown him into. Or his despair at how utterly boring his life was about to become.

Georgina thought he didn't sound particularly enthused by the thought of private practice. There was no pride, no excitement, just an unemotional monotone. She sensed all was not well with this city doctor. 'And how will coming out here help you with that?'

'It won't. But it's a mandatory part of my course and I think it would be quite remiss of me to complete my training without observing one of the world's most experienced ophthalmologists. I think I could learn a lot out here. Professor James and his work are legendary.'

But of course. Another city boy looking for an impressive entry on his CV. She felt stupidly disappointed and cursed the funding-linked government requirement that they provide educational opportunities to tertiary centre practitioners. 'Don't imagine you see much trachoma in the city,' she said.

'It's rare.' In fact, he'd never actually come across a patient with the eye infection.

'Well, you'll see it out here,' she said.

'Still?' he asked.

'It's been largely eradicated, thanks to the prof and his work over the last decade. And we certainly don't see too much blindness occurring from it any more. But we usually get at least one or two kids at each base.'

They continued in silence for a few moments, Andrew contemplating how a disease of the developing world could exist in such a wealthy country. The thought was depressing. In fact, the whole range of conversation since they'd left the homestead had been kind of depressing. Time for redirection.

'What about you, Georgina?' he said. 'Have you always done this kind of work?'

The way he said her name, the way it rolled off his tongue, was disturbingly sensual. It reminded her that under her work boots and sensible clothes she was a woman. 'You can call me George—everyone else does.'

'I prefer Georgina. It suits you.'

'Yeah, well, I prefer George,' she said firmly. Calling her by her full name seemed strangely intimate and that was to be discouraged at all costs. He was putting in his time and leaving—he didn't get such liberties.

He chuckled. *Of course.*

She ignored the laughter. 'I've worked out here pretty much consistently since I completed my training. I've been working with the prof for five years.'

'Ever thought of working in the city? There's a huge nursing shortage at the moment. The hospitals are crying out for experienced nurses.'

Never, ever again. 'I would rather set fire to my hair,' she said.

Andrew laughed out loud. 'We're not that bad, are we?'

Georgina thought about how miserable she'd been so far away from home during her training and how Joel and the whole urban experience had left such a bitter taste in her mouth. 'Been there, done that. Cities are overrated.'

He knew that her blunt statement was supposed to discourage further conversation but it just made him curious. 'Bad experience?' he asked.

'Something like that,' she said noncommittally. 'And, anyway, I'm needed here. I have responsibilities. You think the cities are short of nurses? The bush is worse. The prof needs me, Byron needs me. I'm the can-do girl around here.'

That he'd already figured. And it was actually a concept he understood all too well. Responsibility. People depending on you. It sounded like she was as much a slave to her responsibilities as he was to his. 'Doesn't that get a little old?'

'No,' she said bluntly. It was what she did. She'd been doing it ever since her mother had got sick, before then even. Her mother's illness had followed Jen's death so closely that Georgina had been the one they'd all leaned on. Especially little Charlie. She'd practically raised him. Her family, the prof, they depended on her.

'It must be nice to be so sure about your life,' he said, taking care to keep the bitterness out of his voice.

She laughed. 'Well, I don't know about that. But I do know that this place…' she gestured out the window '…is in my blood. I'm a country girl through and through. I've lived away from it and I never want to do that again. Never.'

Half an hour later George slowed down as she took a rutted track of the main dirt road. 'Nearly there,' she said.

In ten minutes she'd pulled the vehicle up next to a corrugated-iron shack. Kids came rushing out to greet her, delighted smiles on their faces. Several other vehicles were nearby, as well as a caravan with OUTBACK EYE SERVICES painted on the closed door.

Andrew alighted from the Land Rover and came around to join Georgina, who was being swamped by a gaggle of kids all talking at once and calling her name.

They fell back and went silent when Andrew approached, suddenly shy. Their heads bowed and their bare feet shuffled in the dirt.

'This is Dr Andrew,' Georgina told the kids, a toddler already ensconced on her hip.

'Hi,' Andrew said, smiling broadly. He grinned

at the little girl who was snuggled into Georgina's breast. She looked at him curiously and he ruffled her hair.

'Come on,' said Georgina, setting the child down. 'Let's go track down the prof.'

Andrew followed Georgina through the settlement. He'd never seen anything quite like it. It was a mixture of semi-permanent structures, wooden humpies, tents and tin shacks. It was hot, and annoying black flies buzzed around his face. He could smell wood smoke. Dogs and kids watched them pass by and Georgina waved to everyone she passed, calling them by name.

By asking around, they eventually found the prof down at the waterhole, a line thrown in.

'I should have known,' said Georgina, her hands on her hips in mock outrage, to the reclined figure on the bank, hat covering his face. 'Lying down on the job.'

Andrew was reminded of how she'd stood when she'd first greeted him and her wonderful curves. His gaze wandered and it felt so good to appreciate a woman again.

'Georgie girl,' came a deep gruff voice from beneath the hat. The prof removed the object and held out his hand as he sat up slowly. 'Give us a hand,' he said.

George pulled on the prof's hand and accepted his hug, even though she'd only seen him earlier that morning.

'You made it,' he said.

'Of course.' She laughed.

'And this must be Dr Montgomery,' the Professor observed.

'Yes,' said Andrew, putting out his hand. 'Very pleased to finally meet you, Professor James. I've admired your work for a long time.'

Andrew had seen pictures of Harry James but they'd been of a younger man. He was in his seventies now and had aged considerably. He had wild white hair, like Einstein's. And he had slippers on his feet. His shorts were baggy, like he'd lost a lot a weight, and the hem of his T-shirt was half unravelled. Obviously appearances meant very little to the eminent professor.

'Yes, yes,' the elderly doctor said dismissively as he pumped Andrew's hand firmly. 'Now, listen, young fella, you can call me Harry or Prof, like everyone else, but knock it off with the fancy title. It doesn't mean squat out here.'

Andrew laughed at his boss's frankness. 'OK.' He didn't know too many doctors of the professor's calibre back home who rejected their proper titles.

'Georgie girl shown you around?'

'Not yet,' said Georgina. 'Thought I'd introduce him to the head honcho first,' she teased.

Andrew smiled at Georgina's tone. She was obviously very fond of the old man.

'Well, you're an improvement on the last three, that's for sure,' said the prof.

'Thank you. I think,' said Andrew, and earned a hoot of merriment from the prof. 'When do we start work?' Andrew asked.

'Keen, too,' the prof said, nudging Georgina, who just nodded.

Andrew noticed their easy affection. 'I'm looking forward to it very much, Professor Ja— Harry.'

'Goodo,' he said, 'but just relax, Andy, my boy. Tomorrow's soon enough. We're on bush time here.'

Georgina smothered a laugh at the prof's very bad habit of shortening people's names. Andrew Montgomery looked as much like an Andy as the Queen looked like a Lizzy.

'So,' Andrew said, quickly donning his sunglasses as they left the cool shade of the waterhole, 'I'm going to get Andy for six weeks, aren't I?'

Georgina laughed. 'Yep.'

Andrew sighed resignedly. Well, Cory called him Uncle Andy, or used to anyway. These days he didn't call him anything at all—so it wasn't too much of a stretch.

'Will it be a problem?' she asked. She remembered how the prof had called Joel Joe and how much it had annoyed her fiancé.

'Nah.' He shook his head. 'Georgie girl, huh?'

'He's a Seekers fan.' She shrugged and laughed.

'A rock chick and a Seekers fan. Very eclectic.'

Georgina took Andrew on the Grand Tour, a little band of kids following closely behind. She introduced him to Jim and Megan, the two remote community liaison nurses.

'We couldn't do this job without them. They go ahead to the different communities and set up the visits, as well as pull as many people in from the surrounding areas as they can so we can reach as many patients as possible in one hit. They're also responsible for immunisations, general health checks and any other health issues that arise within the communities.'

'So, despite this being primarily an ophthalmic service, it serves as a community health arm as well?'

'Of course,' she said. 'We can't say, oh, no, I'm sorry we don't deal with infected wounds— you'll have to wait for the next caravan in two months' time.'

He laughed. 'I guess not.'

'We treat what comes.'

She showed him inside the caravan next. 'This is where we do the cataract surgery,' she said.

The inside had been converted into a mini operating theatre at one end and a recovery area at the other.

'Tomorrow we'll do all the assessments and the next day we'll operate on those who need it.'

'How many ops are usually done?'

'Depends. Can be only one or two. More normally it's five or six. But back when the service first began, the prof was doing around twelve to fifteen a day.'

Andrew examined all the equipment. He was suitably impressed. It looked like all the latest stuff you'd find in any modern ophthalmic operating theatre. Except he was in the middle of nowhere. Much to his surprise, he felt a frisson of excitement fizz through his veins. His fingers itched to get started.

How long had it been since he'd had that feeling back in Sydney? Months? Years? Doing laser surgery on babies' eyes or on older people with macular degeneration or diabetic retinopathy wasn't really extending him. He'd been bored for a while but denying it because giving up ophthalmology would have been like saying to Ariel that her blindness didn't matter to him any more. And it mattered. Very much. Especially now she wasn't there.

He'd become an ophthalmologist because of her and she'd been so proud of him. He couldn't turn his back on that. It had seemed impossible to change careers when she'd been alive, and now she was dead it *was* impossible. It was even more vital than ever before that he continue in this field. He thought of it as a way of honouring her memory. And turning his back on all the years he had already dedicated to the field to retrain in another specialty just didn't make sense. Not when he had Cory to think about.

But travelling through this wild beautiful land today had had a surprising effect. The primitiveness was inspiring. Maybe there were other ophthalmic options that he hadn't thought about before. His goal of private practice would certainly be lucrative but something like this could really extend him. Give him back the joy and love of his field that had been missing over the last two years. It was still ophthalmology…

He shook himself. How ludicrous! He hadn't even started yet. He could hate it! He could spend all tomorrow bitching about the heat and the flies and his inability to get a decent *lattè*. He looked around at the dirt and scrub outside the caravan window. *Hell, any sort of* lattè!

And then there was Cory. Leaving him for these six weeks had been hard. He'd been through enough this last year without uprooting him to a completely foreign environment. He needed familiarity. He needed stability. Not to be dragged around the outback so his uncle could get job satisfaction. No, Andrew needed to focus on Cory's needs for as long as it took for Cory to navigate the grieving process. AS long as it took to get the old Cory back.

Georgina left the van and he followed her out. 'What now?' he asked.

She shrugged. 'Whatever you like. I'm grabbing my iPod and joining the prof down by the water-hole. I'm sure Megan'll show you all the records from previous visits if you want to familiarise yourself with them.'

'Where do we sleep?' he asked.

She pointed to some tents that had been erected in the distance. 'You sleep with Jim. I'm with Megan. Prof has one to himself.'

'Toilet? Shower? Or do we use the creek?'

'You can if you like. The locals do.' She inclined her head towards the tents. 'There's a chemical loo we drag with us and a bush shower.'

Andrew rubbed his jaw. 'Bush shower?'

She laughed and reminded herself that a cute scar didn't take away the fact that Andrew had probably never camped out a day in his life. 'You're not a camper, are you?'

He chuckled. 'Is it obvious?'

'We fill up a special canvas bag with water that has a nozzle attached to it. It hangs in the sun all day and warms up. You pull on a chain and the water comes out.'

'Sounds interesting.' He smiled.

She rolled her eyes at him. 'Yep. Real adventure stuff out here,' she quipped.

Georgina walked away, shaking her head and trying not to think about how great he'd look standing under that shower. With no clothes on. At least he hadn't said, *How quaint*, as Joel had the first and only time he'd used one. *Whoever had said love was blind had known their stuff. Well, she'd been a prize fool.*

Night fell and Georgina could smell the smoke from the campfire and the delicious aroma of traditional food cooking. Tonight the whole community would attend a coroboree, a feast held in the prof's honour. It was a traditional custom to greet guests with a special meal and Georgina looked forward to these occasions. The ophthalmic team was self-sufficient, always supplying their own food, but this was traditional and they wouldn't insult the locals by not partaking in the celebration.

She'd donned one of the many colourful sarongs

she'd been given over the years by the different communities they had serviced. It was brown and was splashed with bright ochre splotches, a traditional white-dot pattern meandered across the fabric, depicting the course of a billabong. She teamed a brown skivvy with it, the sleeves reaching midway between her elbow and wrist. Even in the height of summer the night air could cool quickly.

Megan and John made room for her in the circle that had formed around the campfire. She was settling herself on the ground when she heard the gruff tones of the prof as he approached. She knew he would sit on the other side of the circle near the elders, as was expected.

He gestured for Andrew to join him and Georgina felt stupidly disappointed. She realised she'd been wondering about him. What he was wearing and how he would look in the firelight. He sat on the ground without hesitation. He didn't request a blanket or a chair or look as if a bit of dirt would be the death of him, like his three predecessors. Like Joel. He just followed the prof's lead and sat.

His eyes met hers across the small circle and she realised that this gave her a great vantage point. *Damn, he was spectacular.* His blondness seemed emphasised by the darker colouring of almost everyone else and the inky blackness of an outback night. He wore faded jeans and a light blue polo shirt and the fire reflected off his face and made the white of that scar even whiter.

As the evening progressed she became so attuned to the deep rumble of his voice, the timbre of his laugh that she barely heard any of the other conversations going on around her. She watched him accept the food offered to him and eat without question. They were eating kangaroo and she savoured the richness of the meat as she watched him accept a second helping.

After they finished eating the haunting sound of a didgeridoo rung out across the circle and silence fell on the group. Some clapping sticks joined in and then the chant of two or three of the elders. Some of the older boys entered the circle, their nearly naked bodies painted in traditional markings. They hopped rhythmically from one foot to the other, shuffling around the circle to the beat, telling a hunting story with their ancient dance.

Andrew watched the firelight glow on the lithe brown skin of the traditional dancers as they streaked by, jerking and twisting to the beat. It was if they had sprung from the very earth. All his senses were heightened. Sitting beneath an umbrella of stars, he could smell the fire and the food, he could hear the crackle of the flames, the music and something more, a primal kind of beat rising from the dirt beneath him.

And he was excruciatingly aware of the woman opposite. The firelight bathed her in a warm glow. It accentuated the streaks of gold in her copper hair and softened her freckles, evening her skin tone until she looked like she'd been polished. She must have applied some lip gloss because her full mouth glistened and beckoned him from across the circle. *How the hell am I going to get through these six weeks without kissing that damn mouth?*

Georgina Lewis, outback tough-girl, had woken his dampened sexuality. He was as surprised by that as he was by the rekindling interest in his occupation. It felt good to be anticipating work and even better to appreciate a woman again. He hadn't realised the power of grief or its full ramifications until now. How much it consumed every part of your life.

The timbre of the music changed and older men, some with beards, took over. Women joined in as well, unashamedly topless, also covered in white traditional markings. Andrew had seen an aboriginal dance theatre once in Sydney, which had been superb. But this performance was breathtaking.

Under a canopy of stars and the glow of firelight, it was a completely spiritual experience.

The dancing continued for a while and when it ended everyone drifted back to the camp and to their beds. Andrew admired the sway of Georgina's sarong just visible in the fading firelight and then fell into step beside her.

'That was amazing,' he said, the awe still present in his voice.

She smiled. 'Yes,' she agreed, 'I love these nights.'

Andrew looked above him and stopped walking. There were never skies like this in Sydney. It was so dark out here he could have sworn the number of stars had trebled. They hung from the night sky as if angels had hung a chandelier in heaven. 'This sky is incredible.'

Georgina stopped too. 'That it is,' she sighed. 'You should camp out underneath it some time. No tent. Just your swag and the sky.'

'I'd like that,' he said, not looking at the stars any more. There was rapture in her face and he could tell she was as awed as he was. He almost didn't breathe for fear of interrupting her concentration and ruining the look.

'I can take you out when we go back to Byron if you like,' she said, a touch dreamily.

'Really?' he asked. A night under the stars with

Georgina? Before he could stop himself he started to think of non-celestial ways to re-create her look of rapture.

Still caught up in the beauty of the heavenly display, Georgina realised a little too late what she had offered. It had been an automatic invitation she would have extended to any visitor, but with Andrew it sounded like… 'Sure,' she said blandly, moving along again, while her heart hammered madly in her chest. Hopefully several weeks of camping out would have cured him of the notion by then.

He fell into step beside her again. 'I don't suppose my mobile's going to work out here,' he said.

She laughed. 'No, city boy, it won't. You'll have to use the satellite phone.'

'OK. It's a little late now, though,' he said. 'I'll use it in the morning.'

'It's only eight-thirty.'

'Way past an eight-year-old's bed time.' He smiled.

Georgina's step slowed. Eight-year-old? He had a kid? *Of course he did, idiot!* The man looked like an Adonis. He was probably married to a gorgeous thin blonde with a gorgeous non-pear-shaped butt. No doubt she worked full time and kept the house immaculate. Just because he didn't wear a wedding ring, it didn't mean that he wasn't married or attached in some way. Or that he didn't have children. And she wasn't interested in this city boy or any other so what the hell should it matter?

'You have an eight-year-old, too?' She tried to keep the squeak out of her voice but really…a kid?

He laughed at the absurd thought. 'No. Cory is Ariel's son.'

'Oh, no,' she gasped, instantly full of compassion for a little boy who had lost his mother. She thought about Charlie and how she sometimes heard him crying at night over a mother he'd never really known. 'The poor kid.'

Andrew swallowed, touched by her empathy. 'Yes, he's taken it very hard.'

Georgina blinked at the need to tell her something so basic. *Well, duh, of course.* He had just lost his mum after all. Georgina had been in her twenties when she'd lost her mother and it had cut her to the quick. 'Does he live in Sydney as well?' she said.

He nodded. 'He lives with me now, actually. I'm his guardian,' Andrew said.

She noticed the slight inflection of doubt in his voice. 'How's that going?' she asked gently. It couldn't be easy for either of them, surely?

'Fine,' he said dismissively. He didn't want to dwell too much on that right now, especially as things weren't really fine at all. Georgina seemed like such a capable person, he doubted she'd understand his struggle to reach out to Cory.

'You must have needed this rotation like a hole in the head,' she said, not believing him for a second.

He chuckled at her frankness. 'It was bad timing.'

'Is he staying with his father while you're here?'

Andrew snorted derisively. 'Absolutely not. Cory's father has been absent all his life.' *Thank God.* Andrew resisted the urge to grind his teeth.

'Oh?' she asked, sensing there was much more to tell.

He felt the old feelings of anger towards his sister's ex mix with his impotence over Cory. Now, this he could elaborate on! 'He was a loser. The first guy she'd ever really opened up to and he turned out to be a slime ball. It wasn't easy for her, you know. Being blind made her really shy and she had trust issues.'

'I can imagine,' Georgina said, trying to fathom the difficulties of having a relationship with someone when you couldn't see them. Couldn't pick up on their visual cues—gauge their sincerity or lack of it.

Andrew could still hear Ariel's broken-hearted sobbing as she had cried herself to sleep every night. 'If I ever see Wendell again, it'll be too soon.'

Georgina shivered at the steel in his voice. 'You sound pretty mad at him.'

Andrew sighed. 'I'm madder at myself. I should have seen him for what he was.'

Georgina wasn't a shrink but she had got the impression over the course of this day that Andrew had a lot of stuff going on beneath the surface.

'You can't be responsible for your sister's choices.'

'Maybe…but I promised my parents when they migrated back to England that I would keep an eye on her, watch out for her.'

'You make her sound like she was some fragile piece of porcelain or fine crystal.'

Andrew laughed. 'Hardly! She was reserved, sure, because of her blindness, but she was fiercely independent. I remember how she dug her heels in and refused to go back to England with Mum and Dad ten years ago. She won, too.'

'So she was her own person. Good. Free to fall in love with whoever she wanted to. Nothing to do with you.' Georgina wasn't sure why, but she couldn't bear to hear him blaming himself over this Wendell. She knew how destructive such thoughts were. 'I guess all you've got to ask yourself is whether he made her happy,' she said gently.

He nodded. 'For a while, yes. I'd never seen her laugh or smile so much.'

'Well, there you go, then. Your sister was happy. That was what you wanted for her, wasn't it?'

'I suppose,' he said. 'Pity there's always a flip side, huh?'

'Amen to that,' she said. She'd been on the flip side and it hurt like hell.

Andrew looked at her, startled by the vehemence in her voice. It sounded like Georgina had been unlucky in love, too. 'At least the worthless rat managed something good. Ariel loved Cory desperately.'

Georgina nodded. 'Sounds like Cory was lucky to have her, even if it was for a tragically short time. Who's he staying with while you're here?'

Andrew hesitated. 'An aunt of mine. My mother's sister. She dotes on him,' he said, feeling the need to defend his choice, Georgina's raised eyebrows and Cory's silent misery flashing back at him. 'She's moved in for six weeks to take care of him.'

An old great-aunt? With a traumatised eight-year-old boy. Didn't sound like a match made in heaven. 'Will she cope OK?'

Georgina had tapped into his concerns with startling accuracy. 'Of course. She's very capable. You'd love her.'

She ignored his jibe. 'And how did Cory feel about that?' she asked.

Andrew saw his nephew's sad blue eyes, so much like his mother's. 'He…understood.'

Georgina looked at him doubtfully. Being so close to a motherless eight-year-old of her own, she could perhaps empathise more with the unknown Cory.

He saw the reproach in her eyes. 'I had to come. They'd already postponed my rotation several times.' He wanted her to understand that it had been a really difficult thing for him to do.

She nodded. She could see how conflicted he was. And this was none of her business. It wasn't her place to judge him.

They reached their tents and came to a halt. Despite the conversation, Andrew had enjoyed the evening immensely. The walk home lit by myriad heavenly bodies had been particularly amazing. He was surprised to discover he didn't want it to end. 'What time in the morning?'

'Clinic usually starts around nine,' she said.

He chuckled. It felt good to laugh after their serious talk. 'I like this bush time. I could get used to it.'

Georgina's foolish heart leapt at the insinuation and she felt herself swaying towards his husky laughter. The walk had been nice. His company more than pleasant. He smelt like soap and she could feel his male heat radiating off him. The temptation to run her finger along his scar was scary in its intensity.

'Don't,' she said, and turned on her heel, fleeing to the safety of her tent while her heart crashed loudly in her chest.

CHAPTER THREE

DESPITE the thunderous noise of the prof snoring for Australia in the next-door tent and very distracting thoughts of Georgina's look of rapture, as well as her look of reproach, Andrew slept remarkably well. The sleeping bag he'd been given was warm without being too hot and the air mattress beneath him was surprisingly comfortable.

The absolute silence of the night took a bit of getting used to. No twenty-first-century noises. No distant echo of traffic, no car horns, no rumble of jumbos overhead. Just the insects that were amazingly loud if he tuned into their frequency and the occasional growl of a disgruntled canine. The odd cough or the sound of a baby stirring. It felt very primitive. Stone age.

Andrew had a sense of how it must have been years ago, before the coming of the white man. Groups of people, families and friends living together. Hunting and food-gathering by day, milling around campfires to talk and eat in the evening. The sense of community was strong out here and for the first time in weeks he drifted off to sleep without a jumble of thoughts running through his head.

He was surprised to find it was eight in the morning before he stirred. He sat bolt upright, listening to the sounds of people going about their daily business outside. Normally he'd have already been on the road, grinding his teeth in the stop-start traffic. He grinned to himself. All he had to do was get up, throw on some clothes, walk out of the tent flap and he'd be at work.

'Morning,' Georgina said, trying valiantly not to drool at his sleep-mussed hair or at the peek of flat stomach muscles she could see as his shirt rode up when he stretched his arms above his head and twisted his body from side to side.

'Sorry, I overslept. It must be the country air.' He grinned.

'Tea, coffee?' she asked, dragging her eyes away from him.

'Coffee. White. Sugar.'

He walked towards her, watching her expertly pull a billy off a campfire, using a stick hooked through the handle. She poured coffee into a mug, added sugar and milk and handed it to him as he approached.

'Thanks,' he said, looking into the mug. It was nothing like the coffee he was used to. There was no froth or smattering of cocoa on top or lid with a convenient hole in it to drink from. A real cup of coffee.

'Sorry, it's not what you're used to,' she said, noticing his frown.

He took a sip. It was hot and milky and sweet and tasted like heaven. A bit like her, really. 'Better,' he said.

She smiled back at him and caught the look of appreciation in his eyes. *Oh, dear.*

'What time did you get up?' he asked, still staring into her honey eyes.

'I'm a country girl, city boy. I'm up with the sun,' she quipped, desperate to keep the conversation impersonal.

Years of shift work hadn't endeared Andrew to mornings. In fact, as far as he was concerned, there was nothing better than a sleep-in on a lazy weekend. He tried not to think about how much fun it might be to convert Georgina to the Sunday-morning treat, especially with her back-off look firmly in place.

'Bacon and eggs over there,' she said, as the look in his blue gaze intensified. 'Help yourself. It's your turn to cook tomorrow morning,' she said, departing the scene quickly as she was finding it a little difficult to breathe.

* * *

By the time the work day got under way, Georgina felt like she'd got herself under control. She had six weeks of this living-in-close-proximity stuff. Working together, eating together, sleeping less than a metre from him. So the man was hot. So they didn't get a lot of hot around these parts. After he was done he'd go back to the city to his private practice and his needy nephew. She'd sworn she'd never get involved with a city boy again, and she meant it. People didn't die from lust and she was an adult.

Some things in life you just can't have. That was one of her father's favorite sayings. And Andrew definitely fell into the 'can't have' category. Oh, sure, they could have a fling because, if she wasn't very much mistaken, there seemed to be a level of interest on his behalf, too. But Georgina didn't think it would be quite that simple for her.

She'd never been one of those girls who could separate sex and love very well. Because to actually sleep with someone it had to be more than just physical for her. She'd had a few lovers but each one had been a serious relationship for her. She really admired women who could be more casual than that. Maybe Joel wouldn't have had such power over her if she'd been a little more nonchalant. More detached.

Joel had been completely dazzling. Her other

boyfriends up to that point, compared to his suaveness and sophistication, had seemed exactly that—boys. She'd resisted at first, not quite able to believe that the best-looking doctor in the hospital had set his sights on her. But he'd been determined and she'd fallen—hook, line and sinker.

She hadn't been young and naïve either, but in retrospect she'd certainly acted that way. She'd been twenty-five. Already a registered nurse and a midwife, and had spent most of her life on a farm with a mob of rough and ready cowboys. She'd gone to Darwin to complete her community health studies and there she'd met Joel, then an emergency department registrar.

And within two months they were engaged and, much as it had broken her heart, she had accepted that her life would be with him, away from her beloved Byron Downs, in a city somewhere. Then a few months later Jen had died and a few months after that her mother had got cancer and she'd moved back home to nurse her during her last months and Joel had acted like a petulant child.

He hadn't cared about her personal pain and grief, or that of her father or her brother and the terrible consequences for little Charlie. Not even the horror and pain of her mother's illness had seemed to register. He hadn't been supportive or sympathetic. In fact, he'd been impatient and sullen. And when he hadn't even made it to Byron for her mother's funeral, he'd totally broken her heart. She'd vowed on her mother's grave that day six years ago that no man would ever take her from Byron again.

And even when she'd been miscarrying his child just a week after burying her mother—her insides shredded, her heart in tatters and her womb achingly empty—she had stuck to her guns. She'd cried a thousand tears over one city boy and she would not do it again.

So falling for Andrew would be gross stupidity. She belonged here. And he belonged in the city in his private practice and with his nephew. And as her father often said, there was no point hankering after something that couldn't be changed.

Andrew approached the day with enthusiasm. He'd spoken with his aunt earlier and her assurances had eased his mind and freed him up to concentrate wholly on what the day brought. He had only spoken briefly with Cory and his monosyllabic answers had been less reassuring, but he seemed no different to any other day, so he hardened his heart and told himself that Cory was getting great care and it was only six weeks and a means to an end.

The prof put him to work with Georgina on the assessments, which he found utterly fascinating. He hadn't given a whole lot of thought to the difficulties involved with accurately measuring visual fields in the middle of nowhere. There were literacy problems so reading letters from a chart wasn't appropriate and a big language barrier, too. A lot of the older folk they saw didn't speak much or in some cases any English, so they had to work with one of the younger community members to interpret for them.

It took a lot of patience and Georgina was absolutely marvellous. Having to stop and explain things to him also lengthened the process. But nobody seemed in any hurry and he was enjoying watching her work. She had a wonderful ability to put people at ease and seemed to be quickly able to get the measure of both the kids and the elders.

She seemed to know a lot of the clients as well, which obviously helped. He had to remind himself that she was one of them. Looking at her, her gorgeous copper curls, honey eyes and wide smiling mouth, he could easily picture her walking out of a boutique in Double Bay, but, as she had told him yesterday, she was a country girl, had grown up not far from here, and that was readily reflected in her ease with these people.

She was polite and respectful and she laughed. A lot. And so did the customers. It didn't matter that they were standing in the sun and it was hot and the black, sticky flies buzzed incessantly. Georgina always seemed to find something to laugh about. Something to make her clients laugh about.

But it was the children she was especially good with. Maybe it was the red hair, maybe it was her easy smile—whatever it was, she seemed to attract little people.

'Have you got kids of your own?' he asked in a brief break. The thought that she might be attached was suddenly disturbing.

Georgina felt the familiar ache inside flare to life. 'Nope,' she said, flapping a fly away a little too emphatically.

He saw the light fade a little from her eyes, surprised by her short, sharp answer. He shrugged. 'You're a natural,' he said.

The ache intensified. 'I have a programme to manage, Byron to oversee. People depend on me. The last thing I need is to add to my workload,' she said, dismissively, calling the next patient forward.

But when Georgina grinned at the gurgling baby on her patient's hip, Andrew had to wonder if there wasn't more to her denials.

Thanks to Jim and Megan, they had about forty people waiting to be processed. They ranged in age from toddlers through to the very old. Georgina did the actual testing, explaining how it worked to each client and adapting her testing to suit each individual's circumstances, and Andrew recorded the results.

Once Georgina had done the visual testing, the client moved on to the prof, who performed the eye exam. It was a bit of a production line but it flowed smoothly. Again, no one seemed to be in a rush and there were no complaints about the length of the queue or elapsed time, like there would have been back in Sydney. He learnt a few tricks from Georgina over the course of the morning and by lunchtime they were halfway through.

After lunch, Harry handed over the reins to Andrew and he examined eyes for the rest of the day, with the prof hovering in the background. He saw it all in just a few short hours. Cataracts of varying degrees, conjunctivitis, blocked lacrimal ducts, some mild glaucoma, a couple of macular degenerations that Jim and Megan would arrange to be seen as soon as possible in Darwin for laser therapy, and his first case of trachoma.

'Ah, so it is,' said the prof, peering into the young boy's eyes through the ocular scopes attached to his glasses. 'We don't see it as much now but when I first started...' he shook his head '...it was rampant. A bloody disgrace.'

The young boy had been complaining of stinging eyes and being sensitive to light. Andrew could see the tell-tale signs of corneal and conjunctival inflammation.

'If we let this go and didn't treat it,' the prof said, 'he'd go on to develop thickening and scarring of the conjunctiva, then his eyelids would turn in and rub against his cornea, which would cause ulcers, and he'd be blind in twenty years. It still happens out here,' he continued. 'And it shouldn't.'

Andrew couldn't agree more when it was so curable and preventable. This little lad was lucky. A course of antibiotics would easily clear the infection by the trachomatis bacteria, yet trachoma was still the leading cause of blindness worldwide.

By the time they'd finished in the afternoon they had five cataract cases for the next day. Andrew found himself very much looking forward to that. It was easy to get used to performing these operations in the vastness of an operating suite with heaps of staff and everything at your fingertips. To do it in a caravan in the middle of the bush would be an unforgettable experience.

All around him the camp was winding down for the day. Georgina was at one end of a rope, chanting a skipping tune as a clutch of giggling girls took turns at jumping the rope. They were all laughing and he found himself smiling as he watched them.

Beyond Georgina he noticed the same group of people he'd noticed earlier. A group of men and women in the distance under some trees, working away industriously. Georgina had told him that they were artists and that a large degree of the community's prosperity depended on their sales of art work—painting and weaving and carved wooden objects. He wandered over towards them now and asked if it was OK to watch for a while.

The dot art was the most fascinating. Jilly, one of the elders he'd been introduced to the previous night, was working on a large canvas, and he watched as she used a short stick with a flat bottom to press a pattern of white dots against the ochre backdrop. It looked beautiful and he thought how much Ariel would have loved to be sitting among such accomplished artists.

'Amazing, isn't it?' Georgina asked, the skipping

finished, also drawn to the clutch of artists. She had a tired, grizzly toddler on her hip to relieve its young frazzled mother, giving her a well-deserved break.

Andrew stood and nodded. 'I wish Ariel was here. She'd have loved this. She'd have been so inspired by the colours out here. She'd be itching to paint it.'

Georgina blinked. 'Paint it? Ariel painted?' she asked as she swayed her hips automatically, rocking the tired infant.

'Ariel was a brilliant artist,' he said. The pride in his voice was unmistakable.

'I didn't think that would be possible, given her degree of vision loss.'

'I know. None of us did. But she did these amazing landscapes. She had this startling accuracy and her work had a real three-dimensional quality to it, like you could actually touch the subject and get a sense of what it felt like. It was almost like she channelled it or something.'

'That's incredible,' Georgina said, watching his face become animated, absently rubbing her chin through the downy fluff of the toddler's head, trying to soothe its fussing.

'It is. It truly is. I mean, everything was just blobs to her, she didn't know what I looked like, what she looked like… She'd never even seen Cory's face…'

Andrew felt the familiar pain and guilt he always felt when thinking about the things his sister had had to endure. As her twin, he had been acutely in tune with her feelings. That she hadn't been able to see Cory's face had torn her up inside. He had often sensed her despair. It just hadn't been right. The one thing that mothers everywhere took for granted, Ariel had been denied. And now she'd been denied seeing her son grow up.

Georgina's instinctual action with the toddler, the swaying and the caressing, was reminding him of how tactile Ariel had been with Cory. How she had mothered him, despite the loss of the most important sense, but had compensated in every other way, being as tactile and physically demonstrative with him as she could.

He cleared his throat. 'And yet the colour and the passion in her paintings was breathtaking. I'd almost talked her into displaying them until Wendell messed with her.'

Ah. Wendell. The ex. Georgina swallowed. No wonder Andrew disliked him so much.

A shout nearby drew their attention away from Jilly and her dot painting. A group of barefoot teenage boys, stripped to their waists, were playing football. Andrew felt his inner rage and frustration at the unfairness of life build. At the obstacles that

Ariel had had to endure in her too brief existence. Why had he thrived and breezed through it all and she'd had every curve ball in life thrown at her? Why had her number been up too soon when she'd had Cory and everything to look forward to?

He felt an overwhelming helplessness threaten to swamp him and as usual it was too scary to deal with. Kicking a ball around seemed like the ideal way to purge the unsettling emotions. Run them off. Tackle them off. Kick them off. Anything but allow them full rein.

'I'm going to go play some footy,' he said.

'They play pretty rough,' Georgina warned him, pulling the infant closer as he began to walk away.

'Good.'

He approached the boys and stood on the sideline watching them for a few minutes. Georgina was right—it wasn't a tame touch match, it was full-on body contact. *Excellent.* Just what he needed for the demons inside him. The ball was eventually kicked his way and he fetched it.

A young lean guy, who looked about fifteen, held out his hands.

'Can I play?' Andrew asked casually, tossing the ball from hand to hand.

'Doc wants to play,' the boy tossed over his shoulder.

Andrew could hear some murmuring. 'Sure thing, Doc,' said another boy.

Andrew grinned and kicked the ball up high in the air and raced after it. The boys didn't give an inch. But he was in the mood for some rough and tumble and, having been a good footballer in his day, he had a feeling that this city boy could hold his own with a bunch of bush kids. And he did. But only just.

Georgina watched the game with the prof from a distance, a now sleeping child lying like a rag doll in her arms. The babe's little body felt heavenly in her arms and Georgina ignored the familiar emptiness inside and concentrated on the game. Andrew had shucked off his shirt so it wasn't that difficult and soon the urge to protect the perfection of his chest took hold. She resisted the impulse to walk amongst all that testosterone and demand that he come away before he got dirty or bruised, or even bloody.

Although he looked pretty good dirty, too. His flat abs and smooth chest was a sight to behold. His arms looked strong and capable and she wondered what it would feel like to be held against him. To place her head in the hollow beneath his collarbone, her cheek against the pad of a smooth pectoral, his flat nipple tantalisingly close.

'He's the one.'

It took Georgina a moment to realise her traitorous thoughts hadn't just been spoken out loud. She blinked and turned to the prof. 'What?'

Andrew caught the ball like he played footy for Australia and ran like the wind. 'He's the one,' the prof repeated. 'Andy. He's the one I want.'

Georgina looked from the prof to Andrew and back again. 'Harry, no.'

The prof dragged his eyes away from the game and regarded his assistant seriously. She never called him Harry. 'Georgina…he's perfect. Look at him.'

She was. God help her, she was. 'We're just a notch on his belt, Harry. He had responsibilities in the city. A nephew back in Sydney who needs him.'

'He's comfortable here. He beats the last three hands down. Look at him with those boys.'

She nodded as three of said boys launched themselves at Andrew's body and tackled him to the ground. 'Don't count on him.' *He'll only break your heart.*

The prof regarded her seriously and nodded slowly. 'Pity.'

Georgina felt the familiar streak of worry grip her. Harry wasn't as young as he used to be. His hair was sparser, his shoulders a little more slumped, the spring in his step a little less obvious.

During the last six months he'd really started looking his age. She'd been so used to his boundless energy and enthusiasm that to see his frailty was worrying.

They watched the game in silence for a few more minutes.

'Georgie girl…I have cancer.'

Even though she'd suspected as much—she'd heard the change in his cough, seen the bloodstained handkerchiefs—to hear the words was still shattering. She nodded and swallowed a lump in her throat that was threatening to overwhelm her. 'I know.'

Georgina struggled with her feelings. She wanted to hug the old man. Tell him how honoured she'd been. How privileged she'd felt, working for him. She clenched and unclenched her hands a few times. Harry James was not dead yet and certainly did not feel comfortable with spontaneous displays of affection. He needed her to be practical. She felt his hand patting her shoulder and it was nearly more than her heart could bear.

'How long?'

'Months. Maybe a year.'

Georgina couldn't bear the thought that all too soon the world would be without a truly remarkable doctor. 'You've refused treatment.'

It wasn't a question. More a statement of fact.

The prof had always been philosophical about death. He figured every day you got was a blessing and when your number was up, your number was up.

'It's OK. I've had good innings,' he said.

Georgina cleared her throat. 'No, it's not OK. There are a million scumbags out there who are going to live until they're one hundred. Why pick on you?'

'Good lord, Georgie girl. Who wants to live that long? I'd just like to find someone who'll carry on my work and then hopefully have some time left over for a bit of fishing.'

Georgina laughed and swallowed the threatening tears. 'I'll get a replacement, Prof.' *If it's the last thing I do. Count on it.* 'You'll get to go fishing.' It just wasn't going to be Andrew.

A couple of hours later Georgina almost got her wish to be held against Andrew's chest when she practically ran into him coming back from the shower. She was backing out of his tent, having fetched something for Jim, as he was entering.

'Whoa there,' he said, holding on to her shoulders as he steadied her from their impact.

His chest was still a little damp and very naked and she had to suppress the sudden wanton urge to press herself back into him. She was acutely aware that all that separated her from his nakedness was one flimsy towel. She stepped away from him quickly and turned around.

'Doing a tent inspection?' he asked.

The towel rode low on his hips and his chest up close was almost suffocating in its beauty, the air in the tent suddenly stuffy. She couldn't help staring at the thin trail of hair trekking downwards from his belly button. Down, down, down…

'Uh…no,' she said, wanting desperately to lick her lips because she was parched but didn't want him thinking she was coming on to him. Because coming on to him would be stupid. *Insane. Crazy. Absurd… Exciting. Thrilling. Tantalising.* 'I was just getting this…' she held up a book '…for Jim.'

He nodded. He could hear a husky note in her voice and thought how sexy it sounded. She was looking at him like a stunned animal in the headlights of a car, and the urge to brush a curl, almost dangling in her eyes, off her forehead was surprising in its intensity. 'Georgina.'

Georgina could see the change in his eyes, the blue intensify, the encroachment of black as his pupils dilated. 'No,' she said, and held up her hand. 'Don't.'

He moved a finger closer to the curl and then winced. The haze of lust that had been descending on him vanishing in an instant.

Georgina frowned as he clutched his right side. 'What?' she demanded, the sexual spell broken. She shifted his hand away with ruthless efficiency, the purple shadow of a fresh bruise starting to darken the flesh beneath his hands. Maybe if she hadn't been so fascinated with his lower abdomen, she would have noticed earlier.

'Andrew!'

'It's OK.' He grimaced.

'I told you they played rough,' she chided, stroking her fingers over the livid flesh. 'Can you breathe OK? Did they break any ribs?'

'Of course I can,' he said, immediately having difficulty as her fingers continued to caress the sensitive area. 'It's fine.'

'This is going to be ten times worse in the morning,' she said, pushing gently as she glared at him. *Bloody stupid boys!*

'Its fine,' he said, gritting his teeth as her fingers elicited a reaction which would not be very easy to hide in his current state of undress. He placed his hand over hers to stop the damn stroking. She had to get out—now!

Georgina looked at him, aware as his hand covered hers that his flesh felt warm and his ribs hard and the ridges between soft and well defined. She could feel the skin beneath her fingers pucker in goose-bumps and felt as if she was trailing fire across his flesh. She dropped her hand instantly. 'You should get Jim or the prof to look at that,' she said, clearing her throat.

'It's fine,' he said again. *Leave. Now.*

'Right,' she said. *Leave. Now.* 'Well…see you later.' She took excruciating care not to brush against him as she left, which wasn't easy in a tent they could barely stand up in.

Andrew breathed a sigh of relief. He'd known Georgina Lewis for just over one day and already going back to the city seemed horribly unappealing.

CHAPTER FOUR

THE next morning Andrew rose earlier, although Georgina still beat him. He'd slept like a log after his energetic game of football, despite the injury. He'd known when he'd landed heavily during a tackle that he was going to pay for it. He thought about Georgina's touch last night and how good her fingers had felt against his skin, and knew he had to get up and get busy or suffer the same reaction as last night.

Georgina was all business. Brisk and brief. She showed him the ropes around the makeshift kitchen and he fried bacon and eggs and cooked beans while the billy boiled. He pulled in some deep breaths of early morning bush air and felt like the swagman in 'Waltzing Matilda'. Like a real man. Like he could do this for ever.

And the feeling persisted throughout the day. The first cataract procedure started at nine o'clock. The prof and Georgina worked as a well-oiled team, a pleasure to watch, and he tried to fit in with them and be as unobtrusive as possible to this routine.

Georgina had already administered the pre-op drops into a snowy-haired elderly woman called Daisy. These dilated the pupil and induced local anaesthesia. Once the drops had had their desired effect, Andrew inserted a cannula and administered a low dose of Valium for sedative purposes. It produced a slight floating effect so that the patient was relaxed and not stressed about being awake while someone operated on their eye.

'I'll do the first one, Andy,' the prof said as Georgina helped him gown up. 'You can do the rest. I think you'll find old Don's interesting.'

'He's the one with the bilateral cataracts?' Andrew asked.

'That's right.' The prof's voice was gruff even behind a mask. 'We'll do the advanced one first. We won't be able to use the newer no-stitch technique, the cataract is too dense. Have you performed any using the old extra-capsular method?'

'Nope. But I'd like to.' He grinned.

'Sure.' The prof chuckled as he snapped his gloves on. 'Figured you'd want to, that's why he's last on the list.'

'When will the other one be done? Does he have to wait an extended period of time?'

'Nah. We'll do it when we head back this way in a month.'

Andrew observed the master and was impressed that a seventy-year-old man had such a steady hand. It felt odd, watching such delicate surgery in such comparatively primitive conditions. But the microscope and the rest of the equipment was as good as any in Sydney and the surgeon—there was none better.

The prof draped Daisy's face and inserted a metal retractor, which looked a bit like it had been made out of paperclips, into the top and bottom eyelids to prevent them from closing. He made a small incision, no more than three millimetres, where the cornea met the sclera. It was so small it wouldn't even require suturing. Then he inserted a small probe into the cut, which vibrated at high frequency and emulsified Daisy's cloudy lens.

'Suction,' the prof requested.

Andrew handed him the instrument and he gently suctioned away the pieces of lens, leaving the lens capsule intact. Next he slipped the new plastic disc-shaped lens into place and the operation was over. In twenty minutes. He secured a cloth eye patch in place with some tape and Georgina ushered Daisy down the other end where there were comfortable chairs and a couch.

Andrew watched her surreptitiously as he and the prof prepared for the next case. She spoke gently and softly and cracked a joke, making Daisy laugh while Georgina took her blood pressure. She made the old woman a cup of tea and popped a plate of chocolate biscuits on the table in front of her.

Georgina poured herself a cuppa and sat down with her patient and went through the post-op information. Andrew saw Daisy's happy smile, her white teeth flashing, and realised he was smiling behind his mask. How different was this work to his normal day? OK, he was still gazing at eyes through a microscope but he never saw his patients post-op like he was now, less than three metres from him. An intimate witness to the laughter and happiness, the anticipation of finally being able to see again. It was so personal.

They did the next few patients over the course of the morning. Another difference to this job. In the city it was get as many in as you could. Schedules and theatre times tight. Here they had a chance to talk with their patients. Spend time with them. They weren't trying for a world record, just delivering a much-needed service while making each patient feel like a person and not a number in a system.

And then it was Don's turn and Andrew felt an excitement he hadn't felt in his job in a long time.

The opportunity to do something new. Yesterday it had been his first case of trachoma and today an extra-capsular procedure.

Andrew was conscious of Georgina hovering nearby as he looked through the microscope into Don's bizarrely white eye. How he'd put up with such restricted vision for so long, he'd never know. That was the one thing that hadn't changed from his city job—giving people back their sight. That was a thrill that never ceased to amaze him. If only he'd been able to give Ariel hers…

Because Don's cataract was so advanced it couldn't be removed through emulsification, Andrew had to open the lens capsule and actually physically remove the entire lens. For this a larger incision was needed and sutures would be required.

He made the cut about ten millimetres long where the cornea met the sclera, opened the front of the capsule and removed the dense, milky lens. He fixed the new plastic lens in place and then worked on closing the incision, carefully placing minute sutures with gossamer thread into the delicate eye tissue.

'Good job, Andy,' the prof said when Andrew had finished the last stitch. 'Couldn't have done it better myself. You're a natural. We could use someone like you out here.'

Andrew looked at the old man, startled, and was

pleased he still had his mask in place. Harry's praise was flattering and for a few moments he allowed himself to indulge in the fantasy of chucking everything in and coming out here and working with the prof, a million miles away from his city problems, and actually getting some job satisfaction for a change.

But Cory…displacing him again wasn't right and he was supposed to be continuing his and Ariel's childhood dream and working with ROP, not some community medicine gig that paid peanuts. He needed to be in Sydney. Cities were where the opportunities were. The good schools. Specialist medical centres. All the mod cons. A chance to earn a decent living for Cory.

Andrew was distracted by Georgina's frown and look of concern. She was worried about the professor. She looked at him and her gaze asked him to let the prof down gently, as she ushered Don down to the recovery area.

'Well, thanks, Harry, you're good for my ego,' Andrew said, reaching behind him, ripping the strings of the mask to remove it and then shaking the old man's hand. 'But where will I go for my *lattè* fix?' he asked.

The prof roared with laughter. 'You do make a good point—no *lattès* within cooee out here,' he said.

He laughed some more then coughed, and within a few seconds was coughing hard, seemingly unable to stop. It had a real paroxysmal quality to it, almost like his larynx was spasming.

Georgina brushed past Andrew, sitting the professor down and passing him a glass of water. 'You OK, Prof?' she asked over his noise.

The old man nodded as he gulped water to ease the pain in his throat. 'I'm good…Georgie girl,' he said, and coughed again, absently rubbing at a spot on his right ribcage. 'Damn nuisance…' He coughed some more but it eventually settled.

Andrew watched as the prof patted Georgina's hand and pushed himself up off the chair. He looked a little grey around the lips and suddenly very tired. Andrew opened his mouth to intervene—the man looked like he needed oxygen—but Georgina glared at him.

'I think I might…go and…throw a line in,' the prof said weakly. 'Thank you, Andy…good job. It's going to be a…pleasure working with you.'

They watched him leave. Andrew was really concerned now about the old man's sudden breathlessness. The weakness in his usual gruff voice was worrying.

'Prof don't sound too good,' said Don from the other end of the caravan.

No, he didn't, Andrew agreed. *Pretty wise for a man who couldn't see.* Andrew caught Georgina's eye and saw the worry there.

'What's wrong with him?' he asked quietly.

Georgina had never seen Harry so frail as just now but she quashed her rising alarm. She knew the prof well enough to respect his wishes on this. He was going to do it his way and he'd earned that right. 'You heard him,' she said. 'He's fine.'

'Georgina,' he said, catching her arm as she tried to walk away.

She saw the concern in Andrew's blue eyes but couldn't bear to discuss it. She looked pointedly at his hand on her arm. 'The name is George.'

She pulled away as he let her go. What the hell did he care anyway? He was going back to the city. To his *lattès*. The prof would die and, no doubt, Dr Andrew Montgomery would sit around regaling his colleagues with tales about having worked with one of the best damn eye doctors on the planet. But Harry James would still be dead and life wouldn't ever be the same.

Andrew made it out of bed not long after Georgina the next morning yet he was still the last one up. He joined her in the open-air kitchen just as she was pouring herself a cup of tea. Her smile was a pleasure to see so early in the day and he realised he'd been anticipating it. She smelt nice and was all bright-eyed and bushy-tailed, and he had the sudden urge to take her by the hand, drag her back to his tent and show her the only reason to be awake at not quite six in the morning.

The sun was fully up but he was unused to such early rising. He yawned and stretched. He usually needed a good shot of caffeine before he felt properly awake. Georgina thrust a cup of coffee towards him, as if she'd read his mind. He raised an eyebrow at her as he took it gratefully.

'You city docs are all alike,' she teased. 'Bears with sore heads until your first hit.'

He smiled back at her over the rim of the cup as he blew at the hot liquid. He liked the flirty sound of her voice when she teased, and was glad she seemed to have recovered from yesterday's incident with the prof—at least on the surface. He took a sip. 'Thanks.'

She turned away from him then and he felt disappointed. The gentle early morning sun bathed her face in a soft light and the desire to kiss her was very strong. This was their third day together and he couldn't remember ever wanting to kiss anybody more. Hell, he hadn't wanted to kiss anybody for so long he'd forgotten how delicious the anticipation could be.

He watched her for a few moments while he sipped at his coffee. She was trimming bacon and it occurred to him as the caffeine started to work its magic that he should be helping. He picked up the frying pan he'd insisted on scrubbing clean yesterday morning and set it on the cooking stand over the fire. He started to crack eggs into a bowl.

'It's my turn today,' Georgina said.

'I don't mind.'

Georgina stopped her activity and blinked as he continued with the eggs. 'I really don't expect you to cook.'

'If I'm awake, I'll pitch in. No biggie.' He shrugged.

Georgina stared after him as he crouched by the fire and dumped the eggs into the pan. *Well, well, well.* An independent male. She'd heard they existed but they were a very rare specimen in these parts. When her mother had died she'd naturally assumed the role of female nurturer and carried it into her role with the prof. Not that her father or John or even Harry for that matter expected it, but they were from a different school out here.

Women's lib didn't enter too many conversations. It wasn't that as a woman she felt her role was segregated to the kitchen—she didn't. But she felt it was her job to make it as easy as possible for the men in her life to do their jobs. It wasn't a hardship. Making a success of an outback life was a team effort.

At Byron she was lucky. They had Mabel, who freed her up to do other things like keep the books and all the other nitty-gritty things that were needed to keep Byron running smoothly. Her father and John worked from sunup to sundown to keep the farm running and she looked after the rest. She or Mabel or both of them together cared for Charlie when John wasn't there, and she mucked in with all the manual messy farm stuff, too, at every opportunity, happy and secure in the knowledge that she was an integral part of the Byron Downs team.

And out here with the prof, she was his right-hand person. Her job title wasn't project manager for nothing. He relied on her to keep things running smoothly so he could do what he did best. Especially these last few months. He was brilliant in many ways but organising was not one of them, which was why he left the day-to-day management of the programme to her. And he certainly couldn't cook to save his life. He had lost weight over the last year and it was one of her priorities to ensure he ate properly.

So to come across a male who refused to be mothered was a unique experience. Every other doctor they'd had there had been more than happy to let her do her thing. And she was good at it. Was proud of what she did. Proud of the eye service and what they accomplished.

She realised she was still staring at him. His back was broad, his legs long, his firm arm muscles flexing as he poked with some tongs at the eggs scrambling in the pan. He chose that moment to look back at her and gave her one of his lazy smiles, and the world tilted. *No. No. No. So the man can cook! Get a grip.*

'The prof not up yet?' Andrew asked as he tipped the scrambled eggs into a dish to keep warm until the breakfast was ready to be served. Like everyone else there, the prof was an early riser, though he had had quite a restless night if the frequent coughing Andrew had heard was anything to go by. Maybe he was treating himself to a lie-in?

Andrew had felt uneasy ever since that incident yesterday. He suspected Harry James had cancer. His cough just wasn't right and the alarming cyanosis he had witnessed yesterday was worrying. And when the prof hadn't joined them for dinner, turning in even before the sun had set, his worse suspicions had been confirmed.

Obviously, from Georgina's warning glare yesterday, it was a taboo subject, but Andrew couldn't help but question the wisdom of the prof continuing as he was.

'I'll check on him when I'm done here,' Georgina said. She had been worrying about the prof's no-show, too.

When the prof still hadn't put in an appearance by the time everyone was digging into breakfast, Georgina slipped away to check on him. Some kind of sixth sense enveloped her in dread as she approached his tent. 'Hey, prof, time to get up, lazybones,' she called out.

When there was no response she lifted a trembling hand to the tent flap and pushed it aside. She could see his still form lying on his side. 'Prof?'

Georgina entered the tent and knelt beside the old man, her heart hammering madly, his stillness frightening. *Please, don't let him be dead.* 'Prof?' she said again, shaking a shoulder this time.

The professor stirred a little at her prod and embarked on another coughing fit, groaning and gasping for air between coughs. Georgina was so relieved to see life it took a few moments to realise that the prof was not looking at all good. His colour was grey and she didn't need a stethoscope to hear the wheezes or his stuttery, rattling respirations. He sounded like he had a lot of fluid on his chest.

She rubbed his arm and waited for the coughing to subside. His skin felt dry and feverish. 'You OK, Prof?' she asked, knowing he was far from it but knowing he needed to come to that conclusion by himself.

'I don't think I can get up, Georgie girl,' he said, his voice a hoarse whisper.

Georgina felt tears prick her eyes as one of the proudest men she'd ever known admitted defeat.

'My chest hurts,' he said, rubbing the same spot he had been yesterday, 'I think…I've fractured a…rib…with all this…damn coughing. I'm not…breathing too good.'

Georgina nodded and squeezed his alarmingly thin arm. She could feel a paltry wasted muscle there and a lot of bone. 'I think it's time,' she said gently.

He nodded at her and squeezed her hand. 'I just need a bit of…a rest,' he said. 'I'll be right…in a week or…two.'

Georgina smiled through the tears shining in her eyes. 'I'll organise it,' she said.

Georgina stood outside the prof's tent for a few moments, collecting herself. She took some deep breaths, steadying her hammering heart. She refused to think what this meant for the prof or the

Outback Eye Service. There were too many things to organise and, no matter what, the prof's work must continue.

Andrew was washing dishes when she approached but her mind was too preoccupied to notice. 'I'm organising an air retrieval for the prof,' she said to him, her voice low. 'Can you go take a look at him? He thinks he's broken a rib. I think he's got some pulmonary oedema and, judging by his fever might be brewing pneumonia.'

Andrew stopped what he was doing and looked down into her honey gaze. He could see a flicker of worry in her eyes that belied her matter-of-fact demeanour.

'Are you OK?' He may have only observed the two of them for a short time but he knew how protective of the prof Georgina was and how deep their mutual respect and affection.

'I'm fine,' she dismissed quickly, before she could be flattered by how nice it was to have someone worrying about her for a change. 'I'll get you to talk to the flying doc after you've assessed him.'

'It's cancer, isn't it?'

Their gazes meshed. 'Yes.'

Andrew watched her walk away, grabbing the satellite phone and positioning herself over near the caravan. She looked so alone over there, with the weight of the world on her shoulders, and his instinct was to go to her, but he knew she'd be glaring at him any second now if he was still standing here, staring at her, instead of being with the prof.

He grabbed a stethoscope out of a nearby medical kit and went to the old man's tent. 'Hey, Prof,' he said, kneeling down. 'Georgina tells me you think you've fractured a rib.'

'Hi, Andy…all that bloody coughing…bound to have.'

Andrew chuckled. 'You reckon you could sit up if I gave you a hand? I'd like to listen to your chest.' He also suspected that the prof would find it easier to breathe if he was upright.

The old man moved onto his back and Andrew helped him into a sitting position. He moved the stethoscope all over Harry's lung fields, listening carefully. It sounded like a symphony orchestra was playing inside. There was decreased air entry on his right side, especially around the suspected fractured rib, and Andrew guessed he had some areas of atelectasis or collapse. Maybe even a pleural effusion, which was quite common in lung malignancies.

The left side was really crackly and he noticed the puffiness of the prof's hands and feet. He pushed at the fluid retention around Harry's ankle and noticed how it pitted. He suspected that there was a degree of heart failure because of his pulmonary insufficiency, causing a systemic backlog.

'How long since you were diagnosed?' he asked, as he pulled the stethoscope out of his ears and pulled down the old man's shirt.

'A year,' the prof said. 'I know, I know,' he said. 'I should never have…smoked.'

'Yeah, well, sometimes we who should know better are the worst offenders.' Andrew shrugged, slinging the stethoscope around his neck.

Georgina rejoined them, kneeling beside Andrew. 'How's he doing?' she asked brightly.

Andrew looked at her fake smile and saw the concern etched in the furrows of her forehead and the fear in the honey depths of her eyes.

'I'm fine Georgie…girl. Much better since Andy made me…sit up.'

Georgina smiled at the prof. He did seem less breathless. She looked at Andrew questioningly.

'I think I'll get a drip in. Do we have any frusemide?' he asked.

Aha, as she'd suspected. Pulmonary oedema. 'Sure, in the van.'

'Let's get him out of here.' He didn't have to say it to her but he wanted the prof where there was a range of emergency medical equipment that could be readily accessed if needed. 'What's happening with the RFDS?'

'They can be at the Burrell strip in an hour,' she said.

'How long will it take to get there?' he asked.

''Bout thirty minutes,' she said.

Andrew nodded. 'Righto. We'll get the prof into the van, give him some oxygen, put the IV in and we'll escort him to the strip.'

'No,' the prof said.

Andrew and Georgina looked at their patient. Because that's what he was now. They had to make decisions for him so they couldn't let their prior relationship with him cloud their judgment.

'You two are needed here…you have to do the post-ops so you won't be late…getting to the next place… Jim or Megan can take me.'

Andrew looked at Georgina. He didn't know enough about anything out here at the moment to know if that would be OK. But he trusted her judgment implicitly. Even after only a couple of days. She nodded confidently at him.

'OK, right. Can you walk, Prof? It's a bit of a hike. We could lift you. I can get Jim to give me a hand.'

'No.' Prof shook his head vehemently. 'My pride is about all I have left at the moment. I'll walk.'

Georgina glanced at him, her eyes begging

Andrew not to dismiss the prof's request. 'The van's too far. I think we'll do worse damage if we let him walk all that way.'

Georgina continued to regard him steadily with her gaze. 'I'll bring the van to him,' she said.

She was gone before either of them could agree or disagree. 'That's my Georgie.' The prof chuckled, instigating another bout of coughing. Andrew passed the prof his pillow and the old man took it gratefully, cuddling it to his chest and splinting his sore rib.

Ten minutes later they heard a vehicle approach and pull up at the front of the tent. When Andrew popped his head out the door, the caravan was probably about two metres away.

'Let's go,' Georgina said to him, springing out of the vehicle, the prof's welfare weighing heavily on her mind.

Between the two of them they helped the prof into the van and, considering they'd known each other for so little time, worked in tandem to get him prepared for his trip to Darwin. Georgina got the oxygen started. The prof's oxygen saturations were only eighty-eight percent and she hastily put a face mask on him at six litres. It only took a couple of minutes to improve his sats to ninety-nine per cent and she noticed Andrew's look of relief mirroring her own as the number improved. He inserted the IV and administered the frusemide as she taped it into place.

'Jim's here,' she said, hearing the engine but not looking away from her task.

The prof put a stilling hand on hers and pushed the mask aside so he could talk. 'I'll be back before Andy leaves,' he assured her.

'Don't worry about us,' she scolded, replacing his mask. 'Right, Andrew?'

He heeded the warning note in her voice. 'Damn straight.' He grinned at the prof. 'You just get yourself better.'

The door opened and Jim's beaming face appeared. 'Your chariot awaits,' he announced.

The prof stood slowly, leaning on the table for support. 'Take care, Georgie girl. Don't let this city slicker dazzle you too much. We need you out here.'

He hugged her and Georgina almost cried at the weakness of the formerly strong embrace. She feigned a laugh. 'Once was enough, Prof.'

'Andy,' he said, releasing her and turning to face Andrew. 'Sorry to leave you in a tight spot. You're a damn good ophthalmologist, you should reconsider your future.'

He held out his hand and Andrew shook it,

feeling each bone of the old man's hand. He dodged the observation. 'It's been an honour, sir.'

Georgina swallowed a lump in her throat as she followed the prof out of the van and into the waiting vehicle. She carried the small oxygen cylinder and passed it to Jim to position as she helped the prof settle into the front seat.

'See you soon,' he said to her.

She nodded and shut the door, hoping with everything she had inside her that the words he'd spoken were true. She had an awful feeling she wouldn't see the prof again.

Andrew stood beside her and she glanced up at him, blinking her eyes rapidly. As she watched the car disappear in a cloud of red dust she felt like she was saying goodbye to her best friend.

'You OK?' he asked gently, putting an arm around her shoulder, seeing the tears she tried to hide.

No. A man I respect and admire is dying. I want to scream and shout and kick things. But his arm felt wonderful and for a second she wanted to push her face against his chest and cry her eyes out. But that was something the capable George Lewis never did.

'Sure, I'm fine,' she said, moving quickly out of his embrace. 'Come on, we can't stand around here all day. We need to shift the van back so we can start the morning clinic.'

CHAPTER FIVE

IT WAS a sombre start to the day and everyone's thoughts were with the prof as they went about their work. Neither the patients nor the staff could believe that after twenty years of being the vital, larger-than-life backbone of the Service, Professor Harry James had shown his first human frailty.

They spent a couple of hours in the morning reviewing the cataract cases from the day before and going through the post-op dos and don'ts and the eyedrop regime that had to be followed for a few weeks. There were no abnormalities and the broad grins from the patients as their eye patches were removed and they could see was a huge buzz for Andrew. It helped ease his concerns about the state of the prof's health.

Don was particularly excited. Andrew had to remind himself that Don, with his bilateral cataracts, hadn't been able to see for quite a few years. The elder shook his hand vigorously, turning his head from side to side and pointing at all the things he could now see again.

'Thank you, Doc, thank you,' he said over and over.

'My pleasure.' Andrew smiled. 'We'll do the other one when we come back in a month.'

Andrew watched Don as he swaggered away, swivelling his head so enthusiastically that Andrew felt sure he was going to give himself whiplash. He was still smiling when he turned to find Georgina standing behind him, grinning madly.

'You did that,' she said.

Andrew heard the slight husky quality to her voice. He shook his head. 'No, the prof did it,' he said. 'He made it possible for so many of these patients to see.'

Having seen the good work the prof did first hand Andrew felt a tremor of apprehension. What would happen to the service now Harry James's future was in doubt? What would happen to it without its driving force?

The next morning Georgina, buoyed by the overnight news that the prof was resting comfortably, watched Andrew surreptitiously as she packed up the kitchen stuff into the trailer. He was dismantling the tents. Jim and Megan had already gone on ahead to the next community at first light so there was just herself and Andrew left to pack up. Thankfully she hadn't had to explain every little detail of the process to him and he'd jumped right in, shouldering the lion's share of the heavy work despite her protestations that she wasn't some swooning female who worried about breaking nails.

He was whistling a tune and she smiled as she realised it was the song he had put up to full bore for her only a few days before. It was hard to believe that it had only been four days. And an eventful four days at that.

Andrew had fitted in so seamlessly. He'd taken the prof's unforeseen departure in his stride. Most city docs found the outback experience hard to get used to and she couldn't think of one from the many she'd known over the years who wouldn't have freaked over being unexpectedly left in charge.

They found it hard enough to deal with the early nights and the earlier mornings and the less than four-star sleeping arrangements. Not to mention the heat, the dirt, the flies, the dark, the quiet. But this one had just eased in like he'd been there for ever.

He bent over to pull out a tent peg and she watched as he stood up, his shirt stretching tautly across his broad back, before bending again to grab another peg. The image of him naked except for a towel that night she had been in his tent arose unbidden and she lost her train of thought for a moment.

She sighed. Damn it all—she was attracted to him. There, she'd admitted it. She shouldn't be. It could never come to anything but…she was. He was sexy and…capable and she was spending too much of her free time fantasising about him. It was time she should have been worrying about finding a replacement for the prof and ensuring the viability of the service after Andrew left.

But she didn't seem to be able to stop. So, she couldn't have him. He was city, she was country. And they both had responsibilities that would keep them in their respective corners. He had Cory, a traumatised eight-year-old nephew, and a promising private practice career, and she had Byron and the prof and the Outback Eye Service, plus her own little eight-year-old nephew, for that matter, who she could never leave either.

He straightened and turned, wiping a hand across his sweaty forehead. He looked in her general direction and she quickly looked down, feigning interest in her packing. If she was going to survive six weeks with her sanity intact, he couldn't know that every time she looked at him her mouth watered. Or when he spoke it reminded her of how long it had been since she'd been with a man.

The Joel experience had shattered her and she was a much wiser girl now. She could recognise a potential Joel when she saw one, and evasive action was the wisest course. Because she'd seen that look in his eyes when he'd given her one of his lazy smiles and it had dangerous written all over it.

'That's it, then,' Andrew said, heaving the three tents into the trailer with a loud thud.

Georgina almost jumped at the noise, so engrossed was she in her evasive action strategy. Be polite. Stay aloof.

'So where are we headed now?' he asked, and took a deep swig of cool water from a nearby canteen.

Georgina swallowed as he threw his head back and she watched the column of his exposed neck, the bob of his Adam's apple and the path of an escaped trickle of water that ran down his chin, over his scar and down his neck. 'A small community called Tulla. It's about two hundred klicks from here.'

'I'll give you a hand with this,' he said, swiping at the errant trickle, leaving a smudge of dirt on his neck, and then wiping his grimy hands on the pockets of his jeans.

'No need,' Georgina said hastily. 'I'm nearly done. You can hitch the caravan to the prof's four-wheel-drive if you're looking for something to do,' she said.

He grinned and she held her breath.

'Sure.'

And he swaggered away.

They made it to Tulla a couple of hours later beneath a leaden sky and unpacked, reversing the process they'd just finished. The humidity was sapping and Andrew was taking a much-deserved drink of cool water from his canteen when Georgina called out to him.

'Phone for you,' she said.

He felt a slight tremor of apprehension as he walked towards the van. Was everything all right with Cory? He dismissed it as he took the receiver from her.

'Reception might be a bit sketchy with the brewing storm,' she said as she left him to it.

He nodded at her and followed her retreat with his gaze as he spoke. 'Dr Montgomery.'

'Andrew, it's Peggy.'

Andrew felt the apprehension return. 'What's wrong?' he asked, his heart beat loud in his ears.

'I don't want to alarm you but…Wendell rang early this morning. He wants to see Cory.'

Andrew gripped the receiver tight. His aunt's voice was fading in and out quite a bit and there was a persistent background hum, but the implications of her statement were loud and clear. A cold fist squeezed his heart and a red haze clouded his vision. *Over my dead body.* He took a couple of deep breaths. Andrew hoped on hope that with the dodgy reception he'd heard wrong.

'He what?'

'He said he has rights.'

Andrew heard the worry in her voice, even through the barely adequate reception. Damn that man. 'Whatever rights Wendell had he gave up when he walked out on Ariel before Cory was even born.'

He struggled to contain the bitterness he felt. The last thing he wanted was to panic his aunt. But no one in the family knew the full story. The memories of that awful night when a distraught Ariel had knocked on his door were still quite vivid.

'What's that, dear? I didn't quite catch what you said.'

'Doesn't matter,' he sighed. The scratchy line was frustrating as hell as Andrew's mind skipped ahead, trying to think of a way to stop Wendell. Damn it, he was in the middle of nowhere. A cloudy day and he could barely even communicate.

'What are we going to do, Andrew? I'm a little worried. His tone was quite threatening,' Peggy said.

'I'm not sure yet. Just let me think for a bit. I'll

get back to you soon. Don't do anything, just sit tight. How's Cory going?'

'He's the same. It's like living with a shadow. He doesn't eat and he doesn't want to go to school. He misses you, Andrew.'

Andrew closed his eyes. Guilt surged through him. Coming out here had been a mistake. 'I'll get back to you shortly, OK? Do not open the door.'

Andrew banged the phone down and raked a hand through his hair. A thousand different emotions crashed around inside him. What kind of a guardian had he been? Cory was still as shut down as he had been six months ago, and he had abandoned the poor kid. And now his good-for-nothing father wanted to add insult to injury.

What can I do? What can I do? Think, damn it! He paced up and down outside the caravan, regretting his trip to the bush for the first time since he'd arrived. How naïve he'd been, thinking it was only for six weeks and that Cory was in good hands. He needed to get back to Sydney.

Georgina approached. She'd been eavesdropping on his half of the conversation and it was obvious something was very wrong. 'Is there something wrong? Is Cory OK?' she asked.

Andrew stopped pacing. 'Wendell's decided he wants to play Daddy.'

'Oh,' she said.

'If he thinks he can just walk back in after… after…'

Georgina heard the barely contained fury deepen his voice. 'After what?'

She sounded so calm and it grated on his stretched nerves. 'After all he put her through,' he said exasperatedly.

'Unfortunately I think you'll find he has rights,' she said again, trying to be the voice of reason in his tangible fury.

Andrew heard her calm reasoning and knew Georgina was right, which made him even crazier. Why was everything so screwed up these days? Why did the courts seem to be hell bent on protecting the guilty at the expense of the innocent? When had parental rights taken priority over kids' rights?

'No. He forfeited his rights when he pushed Ariel down a flight of steps when she was twelve weeks pregnant and told her she was a freak and he didn't want a freak kid. And disappeared, never to be heard of again.'

He sat down on the caravan step and ran a hand through his blond waves, trying to calm down. He wanted to throw something. He wanted Wendell in front of him right now. He couldn't think of a solution like this.

Georgina gasped in horror. She didn't know this Wendell. She'd never met him. But Andrew's fury was obviously well justified. 'So what are you going to do?'

'I'm working on it,' he said.

'Why do you think he's chosen now?'

Andrew snorted. 'Well, as he's never bothered with his kid before, I'd say he's just found out about Ariel's death and has figured there may be some money in it for him.' Wendell had never been keen on working, insisting that it ruined his artistic urges.

'Poor Cory,' she said. She may not have known Andrew's nephew but she knew grief and loss only too well. Her heart still bled for Charlie and her womb still ached for the loss of her own child.

Andrew sat on the step, absently stroking his jaw, his thumb finding the flat, smooth scar. 'I just wish I was there. I feel so impotent here.'

Georgina swallowed as the real meaning of his words slowly seeped in. She thought about how she felt about Charlie and how wild horses wouldn't keep her from him if he was in trouble. Cory needed his uncle.

She took a steadying breath. 'So go,' she said.

Andrew dropped his hands and gazed at her, his eyebrows drawn together, his forehead furrowed.

'What are you talking about?' Andrew had too much on his mind to keep up with this conversation.

'You need to get this sorted, right?'

'I don't renege on contracts,' he said quietly.

She shrugged. 'Well, you'll be the first one. Very few of the city docs make it the full six weeks. No one's going to think any less of you, Andrew. These are extenuating circumstances. You need to prioritise here. Cory needs you.' *How could you have even left him in the first place?*

Her pointed words stung. 'I know that,' he snapped, 'but I'm not walking out and abandoning all of you without a doctor. If the prof was here, I wouldn't hesitate.'

'We'll manage,' she said dismissively.

'Right. I suppose you're going to perform the operations yourself?'

Oh, great, now he was going to play the superior surgeon card? 'I'll get in contact with the department. I told you, we'll manage. I'll organise something. I'm sure we can survive without your brilliance, Dr Montgomery.'

Andrew looked at the colour in her cheeks and the fire in her eyes and kicked himself for his hasty words. He hadn't meant to belittle what she did. Hell, he couldn't think straight! But he sure got her message loud and clear. They didn't need him. She didn't need him. Life out here would go on without him. Even after such a brief time that thought made him strangely sad.

He felt torn. There had to be a way he could fulfil his obligations to both Cory and the job. He didn't want to leave here before his time was up. He'd felt alive again after feeling numb for so long and he was reluctant to turn his back on that. And he knew as he looked at Georgina that it was about more than the job. But then there was Cory…

'Look I'm sorry… I didn't mean… I can manage both,' he said emphatically, his mind busy sorting through his options. 'It'll just take some phone calls and some juggling. I can book them into a hotel as a stop-gap measure—he'd never find them there.'

Georgina listened as he rattled through various options, talking out loud. Not really after any of her input.

'After that I can arrange something more concrete until I get home…'

Home. She felt the impact of the word reverberate through her chest. Having Andrew here, even for four days, had lulled her into a false sense of reality. Just because his transition had been flawless it didn't mean that he belonged here.

'Move them somewhere safer where Wendell wouldn't have a clue—'

'You can't be serious, Andrew,' she snapped.

Andrew stopped abruptly and looked startled at her intrusion, and Georgina was thankful. She was getting dizzy from his rapid spoken-out-loud plans that were getting more desperate, more fanciful as he went along. Had he forgotten that a little boy was at the centre of all of this? His nephew.

'You're going to drag that poor little boy from pillar to post? Hasn't he been through enough?'

Andrew looked at her incredulous expression and the disbelief in her honey gaze. Oh, God, she was right, what the hell was he thinking?

'Look, you know you're not going to be truly satisfied until you can see Cory for yourself. If you don't want to break your contract then take a few days and go h-home.' She couldn't believe how hard it was to even say the word. 'Sort things out personally. Come back when it's sorted if you really feel obliged.'

She was right. These next weeks would be fraught with worry for him. He would spend his whole time torn and preoccupied. He needed to see Cory, but if he did that he doubted he'd be capable of leaving him again. It would mean not coming back, breaking his contract, leaving the Outback Eye Service really in the lurch. Not to mention jeopardising his position in the ophthalmology programme. And his chances at a lucrative career.

'Hell, pack him up and bring here for the rest of your contract. Wendell will never find them out here,' she said.

Andrew blinked. 'What?'

The suggestion came from out of the blue but the more Georgina thought about it the more sense it made. If Andrew insisted on fulfilling his contract, his mind wasn't going to be on the job if he was constantly worrying about Cory. Then she may as well have no doctors for all the good he'd be. But if Cory was safe with him?

'Bring him here,' she said again, smiling this time because she was liking the idea more and more.

Andrew stared at her stupidly. That was the most preposterous thing he'd heard in a long time. 'Are you crazy?'

Georgina laughed at the stunned look on his handsome face. She shook her head. 'Think about it,' she said, moving in closer to him, touching his forearm with her hand without conscious thought. 'Cory will be safe here with us. Thousands of miles away from Wendell. You won't be worrying about him. And he'll love it. Trust me, I grew up out here and every day is like an exciting new adventure.'

'No.' He shook his head, the idea worming into his subconscious even as his practical side rejected it. 'It's hardly very professional, having my nephew come along for the ride. It must break every rule in existence. And then there's his schooling.'

Georgina shrugged. 'That's the beauty of working out in the sticks. We can be more relaxed about the regulations. And if we rearrange the scheduling we should be able to hold the clinics at Byron in a week or so—we've done that before—which means that Cory can do School of the Air with Charlie.'

Just like that? 'I'm sure the last thing your father and brother need is a three-ring circus moving into their front yard and a morose eight-year-old.'

'They won't mind.'

'You haven't even asked them,' he said. Was she really serious? It sounded so crazy.

'Hey, city boy, that's the way things work out here. If someone's in trouble, we all pull together. Byron is my home, too. I don't need to ask permission to have guests come and stay.'

Andrew hesitated. 'But it'll be an unfamiliar environment for Cory.'

'No more unfamiliar than all the convoluted planning you were just talking about. And anyway—you'll be with him. You know that's all he really needs, right?'

'Yes, of course, but he's a city kid—'

'Charlie'll show him the ropes.'

'He's not very social at the moment. He's…difficult.' The last thing Andrew wanted was to upset Charlie by Cory's sullenness.

'Of course we'll all make allowances. Mabel will love it, she adores kids. She'll be great for him. I've seen her woo the surliest of children.'

Mabel? 'Mabel has got to be at least seventy.'

Georgina shrugged. 'Seventy-one. She won't mind.'

'I think asking a seventy-one-year-old woman to cope with a newly orphaned child is a huge imposition.'

'Are you kidding? She'll thrive on it.'

Part of him wanted to say yes very badly. It would be the best of both worlds, and just thinking about Cory roaming free out here was enough to put a big country smile on his face.

Georgina could see him swaying. 'Look,' she said, touching his arm again, 'I get it. We'll have to tread carefully with Cory. But it's only for about five weeks. This is a really good idea and you know it.'

He sighed. She was right. He could feel the excitement as her enthusiasm started to infect him.

He'd never relax out here, knowing Cory was vulnerable. And having Ariel's son by his side would feel so right. Abandoning him even with quality care and the best of intentions had been wrong. He wanted to make it right again. For Ariel. For Cory. 'Yes, all right, it's a good idea.'

She grinned at him and almost gave him a hug. 'But of course.'

'All right,' he said. Why not? 'What the hell. I can't promise it'll all run smoothly but…thank you. I'll organise it now.' *Before I change my mind.*

'Give me your aunt's details and I'll do it,' she said. 'You go and catch up on tomorrow's cases with Jim and Megan.'

Andrew regarded her seriously. She was so used to being the one who organised stuff she didn't even realise she went above and beyond her job requirements. 'Is that how it usually works, then? You just take over, shoo people away and they just let you do it?'

Georgina looked at him, slightly puzzled, and blinked. 'That's what I do around here. Organise things.'

'Even when someone's perfectly capable of doing it themselves?'

'In my experience, it's just easier and quicker to do it myself. And I know it's done right.'

'Don't you get weighed down by being the one everyone depends on?'

She shrugged. 'I know my strengths. I'm right-hand girl. I know it wasn't just my nursing background but my organisational skills that got me this job. I know the eye service and Byron run smoothly because of me. I know stuff that the prof and Dad and John don't know. I know how many lenses to order, I know who to ring if the generator breaks down, I know how to do the payroll for both. I know how much grain to order in the dry season, I know…where the mousetraps are kept and how to produce a computerised statement. If I don't know these things then nothing functions.'

He nodded. She'd made herself indispensable to everyone. 'Thanks, but I can manage. All I need is a Darwin phone book.'

'Well, lucky for you I know where the phone books are kept also.' She turned and opened the caravan door, retrieved the book and handed it to him.

'My job may seem trivial to you, not as important as delicate microsurgery on an eye, but without what I do, this team wouldn't function.' She brushed past him.

He shot a hand out and stopped her. 'I don't mean that. I mean people use you when they're perfectly capable of doing things themselves. You spread yourself too thin. I've watched you here, trying to be everything to everyone, juggling too many balls. You're going to burn out. You're an enabler. You're nurturing their helplessness. What happens when you leave?'

'I'm not leaving. Ever.'

Her bullheadedness was frustrating. Out of sheer desperation he said the first thing that came into his head. 'What if I asked you to come to the city with me?'

Georgina felt her eyes widen as his statement hit her. Her heartbeat roared in her ears and pounded in her chest. 'Don't.'

Half an hour later he'd organised everything. The clouds had blown over, which made communication much easier, and he'd practically burned up the satellite. Peggy was taking Cory to a hotel after school and they were flying to Darwin first thing in the morning. He'd chartered a small plane from the Darwin airport to bring them to their nearest airstrip, about half an hour from Tulla, and he would be waiting for them. Peggy would return with the pilot and continue back to Sydney.

He felt very accomplished when he replaced the phone after speaking to Peggy. And not so worried any more. Of course, he wouldn't totally relax until he saw Cory tomorrow afternoon but at least he felt back in control.

'Well?' Georgina asked as Andrew joined their case meeting a little while later.

She ejected the tremor from her voice. She would not let him see that his earlier throw-away comment had totally thrown her for a loop.

'Cory will be here at three tomorrow afternoon.'

And he grinned at her, a smile of such relief and happiness that she grinned back, despite the very strong sense that everything was about to change.

Next morning Andrew zipped through the morning stream of patients as Georgina finished with their acuities. There were two cases of trachoma at Tulla and Andrew met his first adult who had been blinded by the infection twenty years ago. The elder had presented for a routine vision check. He had a very supportive extended family and Andrew marvelled that a person with his disability could not just live but thrive out in the bush away from any of the essential services that could be found in cities.

He whistled through his workload and answered questions about the prof and tried not to be too distracted by Georgina, who was wearing a broad-strapped navy singlet with her cargo pants. Her arms were bare and her coppery curls brushed against them and her laugh carried to him constantly on the light breeze.

Every time he turned around there seemed to be a little one attached to her. Either on her hip or wrapped around a leg. It was nice, watching her with them. She lost the tough-girl façade and he could see her gentleness, her compassion. It gave her a whole different appeal and one more reason for him to steer well clear. He did not have time in his life for relationships.

Before he knew it, it was time to pick up Cory and he felt a queasy feeling in the pit of his stomach, worrying whether or not he'd done the right thing. Georgina was right—the boy had been through enough. Would he look at him with those same silent betrayed eyes as he had when Andrew had left? He hoped not. He hoped his decision to come out here hadn't caused any irreparable damage.

'It'll be fine,' Georgina said, the silence in the vehicle stretching her nerves. Andrew was sitting upright, one hand grasping the armrest on the door, the other holding onto his seat belt where it crossed his chest. She could sense Andrew's growing apprehension and it was rubbing off on her. Her heart thudded loudly in her chest.

She gave his arm a squeeze, a purely reassuring gesture, and beamed a positive smile at him. He returned her smile with less gusto and removed his grip from the seat belt, absently stroking at his scar.

Georgina was glad to get to the outback strip—the same as Byron's, the same as all the ones in the back of beyond. A raised, cleared stretch of red dirt. The sooner the reunion happened the better, as far as she was concerned. The tension emanating from Andrew couldn't be good for his health.

They sat together, companionably silent on the bonnet of the vehicle, Andrew peering into the endless blue of the sky, eager to spot a first glimpse of the plane he had chartered. In the end he actually heard it first. Then Georgina did, too, and they both scanned the sky expectantly.

'There,' she said, spotting it first and pointing to a tiny speck in the distance.

Andrew breathed a sigh of relief. It was actually happening. Cory would be here soon. It grew larger quickly and minutes later it was landing. He pushed himself off the bonnet and stood holding his breath as the door opened and the steps lowered.

Peggy climbed down first, waving and smiling at him. Andrew walked towards the plane and watched as his aunt turned and helped Cory down the steps. He felt his heart swell in his chest as his nephew placed his small hand in Peggy's. He looked thin and fragile and pale.

Genetics had played some role in that. Ariel had been delicate with a fine bone structure and had looked a bit like a puff of wind would have blown her over. Cory had always been a finicky eater but he had dark circles under his eyes and looked like an old man instead of eight. Andrew shut his eyes briefly, feeling worry gnaw at his gut. *How can I help him?*

He gave his aunt a huge hug. 'Thank you for doing this,' he said quietly in her ear.

She smiled at him as she pulled away. 'Aren't you going to say hi to your uncle, Cory?' Peggy asked, looking down at the little boy who was standing silently by her side, eyes downcast as if the red soil was the most fascinating thing he'd ever seen.

'Hi,' Cory said in a small voice, not bothering to look up.

'Hey, mate,' Andrew said. He didn't know what to do next. He wanted to hug him but his nephew was emitting very strong non-verbal don't-touch-me cues. Should he do it anyway? He didn't want to push Cory. He'd been waiting patiently for the last six months for Cory to trust him, not crowding him, giving him time and space to realise that his uncle was there for him.

He settled for ruffling his hair and pulling Cory into his body for a quick squeeze. He was conscious of Cory's stiffness and the fact that his nephew's skinny arms didn't creep around his waist like they used to before his mother's death.

Georgina watched the whole exchange, horrified. She had never seen a child look so alone. They may as well not even been here. He looked like he would have been perfectly at home standing on the landing strip in the middle of nowhere by himself. A tiny dot in the vast landscape.

He was too pale, too thin, too emotionally stunted. He looked like he'd just walked out of solitary confinement. And every maternal instinct she possessed cried out for him.

'Cory, this is Georgina,' Andrew said.

'Hi,' he repeated, again not looking up.

Georgina looked from Peggy to Andrew and then back to Cory. She got down on her knees in front of him and swept the boy into her arms. Their heads were level and she stroked his hair as she held him tight. He was stiff in her arms but she didn't care. If ever a child needed a hug, it was Cory. She felt him relax against her after a few seconds and she swallowed a lump in her throat. 'You can call me

George,' she said to him, as she reluctantly ended the embrace.

Andrew watched, amazed at Georgina's easy display of affection. He'd been too afraid Cory would crumple if he pushed too hard or took things too quickly. But Georgina had just dived right in.

'You must be Peggy,' Georgina said, rising from the ground, uncaring of the two patches of red dust clinging to the knees of her cargos. 'Nice to meet you.'

'Likewise,' said Peggy, taking Georgina's hand.

'Well, come on Cory, let's get you settled in the car,' said Georgina briskly. 'Your uncle can bring your stuff.'

She smiled at the boy and he fixed her with a mournful stare. She held out her hand to him but he ignored it. She kept smiling at him and reached for his hand anyway, enclosing it in her own and pulling gently as she strode to the vehicle.

Peggy and Andrew watched them go. 'She may be just what that boy needs,' said Peggy appreciatively.

'He needs his mother,' Andrew said, wondering if his aunt was perhaps right.

'Or a damn good substitute,' she said, as she kissed him on the cheek and turned back to the plane for her return trip.

CHAPTER SIX

GEORGINA kept up a steady stream of chatter as they drove back to Tulla. Andrew sat in the back with his nephew and followed her cues, but Cory seemed more interested in staring out the window, and all they got out of him were monosyllabic replies. Andrew's frustrated gaze met Georgina's in the rear-view mirror and she smiled and nodded at him encouragingly.

They arrived and Andrew took Cory on a grand tour. He had hoped that Cory would be excited about camping out in a tent but the boy just nodded solemnly when he showed him where they would sleep. He was polite to everyone he met, the good manners ingrained into him by his mother evident, but he showed no real interest in anything.

The Tulla kids were quite fascinated by him. A few of them tried to include him in their trip to the local waterhole for a swim but he politely refused. Andrew dragged him into a game of cricket but he showed no enthusiasm at all in the outfield. His moves were very mechanical, disinterested, as if he'd rather be anywhere but where he was.

'Can I go now?' he asked his uncle after twenty minutes, and Andrew nodded miserably and watched the forlorn little figure walk back to the main camp area.

Georgina spotted him as he wandered back in. She was again struck by his isolation. He looked like he had an invisible shield around him. She guessed he wore it to keep from being hurt again, but it also kept all his misery and pain and hurt inside as well. He sure as hell needed an outlet for that before he was permanently damaged.

She noticed him watching a group of locals. They were sitting in a nice shady spot and had formed the usual afternoon circle of artists that could be found in most camps. They were chatting and laughing as they put paint on canvas.

'Hey, Cory,' she said, approaching him, 'you want to go and watch?'

Cory looked at her, startled, and shook his head.

'Nonsense,' she said, grabbing his hand as she had earlier at the strip, and led him over. 'Archie and the gang love an audience.'

She introduced Cory to the five elderly artists and pulled him down to sit beside her. She could see he was instantly fascinated, his gaze following each and every stroke, a small light glowing in his eyes. His uncle's eyes. His mother's…she supposed.

After about twenty minutes Archie looked at Cory and said, 'You wanna go?'

Georgina expected him to refuse, to withdraw, but much to her surprise he said, 'Yes, please,' in his small polite voice.

Archie gave Cory an impromptu art lesson and she could see his little hand trembling as he made his very first stroke against the canvas. He blinked as if the bold orange ochre slash had been made by somebody else and then looked at her with his solemn blue eyes. A ghost of a smile fleetingly turned his pale lips upwards. She smiled back at him and knew in that moment that Cory was going to be OK. He'd found his outlet.

The next morning at breakfast Cory did his usual not-hungry act. Georgina watched as Andrew tried to coax him into eating something—anything— and Cory finally nibbled on a dry piece of toast.

Georgina could sense Andrew's frustration and could see how Cory's distance and isolation were breaking Andrew's heart. She dished up a small bowl of scrambled eggs and sat next to Cory.

'Here, mate,' she said, 'get these into you. Do you

think your mum would want you to stop eating?'
She heard Andrew's harshly indrawn breath but
ploughed on anyway. 'If you want to be an artist like
your mum then you need to feed your body so you
can feed your muse. You know what a muse is,
Cory?'

The little boy shook his head. 'It's that thing deep
inside…' she tapped his chest '…that inspires your
artistic soul. Your mum had one, I bet. Your uncle
told me all about what a great painter she was and
all great painters have them. And muses are hungry
little blighters. So eat up and you can paint with
Archie again today.'

Georgina finished her little speech and looked up
at Andrew, happy with herself. Andrew, however,
was not. His blue eyes were chilly and his mouth
was flattened into an unimpressed line. 'Can I talk
to you in private for a moment?' he said, standing
and stalking over to the caravan.

She looked down at Cory, who was swallowing
a mouthful of food. He looked worried and she
smiled and winked at him. 'Great going, Cory.
Keep up the good work. I'll be back shortly.'

Georgina took her time walking over to where
Andrew stood glaring at her. She needed to prepare
herself mentally for this confrontation. She had
interfered where it wasn't her place, but she'd

watched Andrew with Cory enough to know that he was trying to do his best but going about it all wrong.

'I'm sorry,' she said, hands out, tone placatory, 'I didn't mean to butt in. This is none of my business.'

'Damn straight, it's not,' he snapped. 'I don't want you mentioning his mother like that.'

Huh? 'Why not?'

'It took two whole months to stop him dissolving into tears every time his mother was mentioned.'

Huh? 'Well, she's dead. Of course he cried.'

'It was heart-breaking,' Andrew said. His gut still churned when he thought about little Cory's anguished tears. He was supposed to be looking after Cory, making him better, not making him more miserable.

She had no doubt, her own family's grief still recent enough to know how devastating it was. 'It's natural. It's…normal.'

Andrew raked his hand through his blond waves. 'I'm trying to get him through this,' he said, exasperation tinging his voice.

'By denying Ariel ever existed?'

'Of course not,' he snapped. 'But I just don't think encouraging him to paint is going to help him get over his loss. All it's going to do is remind him of his dead mother.'

Georgina heard the crack in his voice and had to remember that Andrew was also grieving for Ariel. His sister. His twin. He was damaged by Ariel's death as well. Was it fair to ask a grieving man to fix a grieving child? Surely it was like the blind leading the blind.

She looked at him absently stroking the scar on his jaw. A man she was already too involved with emotionally after such short acquaintance. A city doctor way out of his depth with an eight-year-old grieving boy who depended on him. She saw how eaten up he was by his relationship with his nephew and even though her sensible side urged her to exercise caution, it had never really been her way. She tended to speak her mind. It was the way of things out in the bush.

She sighed. 'You are going about this all wrong.'

Goddamn it, he knew it wasn't working, but did she have to be so blunt? 'Oh, so now you're a child psychologist as well?'

Georgina refused to let his sarcasm get to her. 'No. Just someone who possibly knows a little more about eight-year-old boys and raising a child than you do.'

OK, good point. 'Look, I'm sorry, that was uncalled-for,' he said, rubbing his eyes. 'I'm doing the best I can.'

'Of course you are,' she said quietly, and touched his arm. 'But I think you're too close to this to really see what's best. Cory lost his mother, yes, but you also lost your sister. It must be hard for you, too. You haven't had time to grieve for Ariel because you've had Cory to worry about.'

'I'm fine,' he dismissed.

OK, sure. 'Then why can't you hug him?'

Her simple question blasted into the space between them, defeating him. Andrew had despaired over this often enough. It wasn't that he hadn't tried, he'd just given up. It had so obviously made Cory uncomfortable and he was worried that pushing him would scare him away. It hurt that his formerly affectionate nephew now rejected any of his comforting overtures. He shrugged. 'He doesn't want me to. He doesn't like it.'

She snorted. 'He's eight. Of course he wants you to. Of course he likes it.'

'I'm trying to give him space and time.'

'Are you? Or is it just too hard for you to hug him and have him around because he reminds you so much of Ariel? Of the sister you love and miss just as much as Cory does?'

Andrew looked at her, opened his mouth to deny her accusation, but the words wouldn't come. What if she was right? He stopped pacing and sat down on the caravan step, by habit his thumb finding the scar. God, had he been keeping his own nephew at arm's length to protect himself? 'He does remind me of Ariel. So much,' he admitted quietly.

'Yeah. And I'm betting that you remind him so much of his mother, too. I mean, I assume that as you were twins you must have looked alike.'

Andrew nodded. He pulled out his wallet and passed her a small photo. It was picture of Cory, taken a few years ago, with Ariel. She almost gasped, the similarities were so striking. Ariel was a female version of her brother. As femininely beautiful as Andrew was masculine. Long blonde wavy hair, high cheekbones, the same crystal-clear blue eyes, although they had a certain unfocused quality, due to their blindness, she guessed. Ariel had a kind of ethereal quality about her. She looked fragile but there was something about the way she held herself that belied the frailty of her features.

Georgina shook her head, staring at the photo. 'No wonder,' she said.

'What?'

'No wonder he rejects your comfort. You look just like her. The poor kid's trying to protect himself.'

Andrew looked at her as she gazed mesmerised almost by the picture she held in her hands. 'From what? Why?'

'From losing another version of his mother.'

The words fell between them and her logic made something that seemed so complicated sound so simple. Was she right? If so, he'd totally stuffed it up by going and doing exactly as Cory had feared—he'd left. 'So how do I fix it?'

Georgina noted the anguish in his tone. Andrew was asking her for help and she fleetingly thought about rejecting him. She didn't need their emotional baggage as well as her own. There were five more weeks and then Andrew and his nephew would be gone so why get too involved? But could she turn her back on Cory? A little boy, just like Charlie? Her derailed maternal instincts were telling her she could help them to find each other while they were there, send them back to the city in better shape.

Maternal instincts that had never had a chance to fully develop. Instincts that had been looking for a home since her miscarriage shortly after her mother's funeral. Instincts that had found a home in her little patients and Charlie and now Cory.

She sighed. 'I don't know, Andrew, but not by avoiding issues. Not by tiptoeing around and pretending his mother never existed or denying him this sudden artistic flair. Yes, he needs a lot of extra support at the moment, but he's still just a little boy.

One who's hurting a lot and is finding some kind of therapy in painting. The canvas he painted yesterday is very good.'

Andrew shook his head, still shaken by what he'd seen. 'It's so dark.' Ariel's art had been full of colour and light. He could still see the dark black heart in the ochre background.

'It's what he's feeling, Andrew. We can't deny him that outlet. He's obviously inherited a gift from his mother. We should be encouraging that. And you should be hugging him, Andrew. Every chance you get.'

'And if he keeps rejecting me?'

She shrugged. 'Hug him more,' she said. 'He'll get used to it and one day soon he'll hug you back.'

Andrew looked at her doubtfully, too many vivid memories of holding a reluctant Cory uppermost in his mind. 'Promise?' he said, and gave a half-laugh.

'Cross my heart,' she said, doing the action.

Andrew followed it. Their gazes locked. And Andrew knew without a doubt that it had been his destiny to come here and meet Georgina. That they had crossed paths so she could make sense out of something he was too close to to make sense out of himself. Maybe Peggy had only been half-right. Maybe Georgina was just what he needed, too?

* * *

The next afternoon, after surgery had been completed, another cricket game got under way. Cory, who had moved around the camp all morning, dragging a canvas with him, was now happily ensconced amongst the camp artists. Andrew had tried to coax him into joining the game, fretting that he had taken to a rather solitary pastime, but Georgina had shaken her head at him subtly and was relieved when Andrew had let it be.

She dragged a chair over to the shady spot Jim had claimed, and sat down. From here she could keep an eye on the game and Cory. A little boy wandered over and handed Georgina a banana. 'For me?' She smiled.

The child shook his head silently, his solemn brown eyes never leaving the banana.

Georgina laughed. 'Ah, I see. You want me to peel it?' she asked.

She was rewarded with a white gappy smile and her heart lurched and she ached deep inside as she dealt with the skin and wondered for the millionth time what her child would have looked like. Would it have had the Lewis colouring or been darker, like Joel? Have the same coloured eyes as this little boy?

She broke the peeled banana in two and handed it back to the child. He gave her another smile and she watched as he toddled away, munching merrily. She heard a shout from the game and quickly reined her emotions in. Some things just weren't meant to be, she lectured herself as she returned her attention to the match.

As with any sport that was going, Andrew was in the thick of the action. Two garbage bins were used as wickets and the handle on the bat was looking a little the worse for wear.

'George,' Jim said, 'watch this kid.' He pointed to the skinny lad that was embarking on his run-up to bowl. 'Fourteen years old and can bowl like no one I've ever seen.'

Georgina rolled her eyes but followed the path of the incoming bowler. She didn't know a whole lot about cricket but as the hard red ball cannoned out of the boy's hand and whizzed down the pitch at a cracking pace, completely bamboozling the younger batter, she had to admit he was good.

She whistled. 'Very impressive.'

'I'll have to see if Andy has any contacts in the city to get a selector to come out here. With the right training he'd be an ace for the Australian team,' Jim said.

Another ball shot down the pitch and Georgina winced as the batman ducked to protect his head. 'Do you think they should be playing without headgear?'

Jim chuckled. 'Of course they shouldn't. Good luck convincing them, though.'

Andrew, who was in the outfield, was thinking the same thing. He saw Georgina's wince and decided to move closer, maybe suggest that the bowling whiz take it a little easier, but the ball was handed to someone else and he relaxed. That kid was amazing.

In one week Andrew had played more sport than he'd played in the last two years. At lunch and after they'd knocked off for the day there was usually something going for him to join in. Rugby league and Aussie Rules was popular but he'd also played basketball, baseball and soccer.

Andrew's gaze kept wandering to Cory. He could just see his nephew's downcast head, his fair hair and pale skin a vivid contrast to the locals'. He had certainly embraced painting and Andrew chewed on his bottom lip, hoping, as Georgina insisted, that it was a good thing.

The ball whizzed past him and the boys yelled at him, mostly in some native language, and he smiled to himself as he retrieved the ball. Fair enough. His mind had been elsewhere and he'd missed an opportunity. And these kids took their cricket seriously. He noticed Georgina laughing at him as he threw the ball back to the wicketkeeper and he smiled and shrugged his shoulders at her.

A few minutes later another wicket was claimed then a certain hush fell over the makeshift red-dirt field. A young lad came up to bat and the ball was immediately passed to the bowling whiz. Andrew felt the hair on his arms prickle. He saw the two boys grinning at each other from either end of the pitch. These two were obviously old rivals.

'Get closer, Doc,' the kid beside him said. 'Bobby's gonna smash Dazza all over the pitch.'

And so it began. The two boys were evenly matched—Bobby brilliant with the bat, Dazza equally skilled with the ball. They were rivals, yes, but friends too, if their good-natured banter was anything to go by. Andrew had been worried about what damage Dazza could do with that ball, but Bobby more than knew how to handle a bat so Andrew relaxed.

Unfortunately, though, after twenty minutes of the most riveting amateur cricket Andrew had ever had the pleasure of watching, Bobby misjudged a ball. Andrew, who was quite close to the action, watch in horrified slow motion as a speeding cricket ball slammed straight into Bobby's left eye. He dropped, as if he'd been shot, screaming in the dirt, clutching his face.

Andrew was at his side in seconds. Georgina arrived seconds after that, with Jim a close third. Bobby was in so much pain he wasn't even trying to be brave in front of all his friends. He was howling his lungs out.

Andrew hauled the boy upright and pried his hand away from his face. 'I need to look at it, mate,' he said, as the other hand came up to take its place.

'Bobby, Bobby, sorry.' A distraught Dazza added to the crowd of bodies around the scene. 'I'm sorry. I didn't mean to hit you…Bobby.'

'Come on, now, Dazza,' said Jim, pulling the boy away from his friend's side. 'All of you, give Andy some room to work.'

Andrew was thankful for the space and some relief from the excited chatter of voices all round him. Georgina held one of Bobby's hands so Andrew could examine the injury.

The eye was already swollen shut and was continuing to increase in size as they watched. A livid purple bruise, ringing the entire orbit, was also appearing before their eyes. Georgina winced and looked at Andrew.

Jim crouched down beside them. 'Nasty.' He whistled.

Andrew pushed gently around the orbit and

zygoma. 'I think he's fractured the cheekbone as well as the orbit. The swelling is dramatic. I wouldn't be surprised if he's ruptured his globe.'

'He's going to have a hell of a hyphaema,' Georgina added, barely even able to look at Bobby's injured eye.

'That he will. And a good dose of glaucoma to go with it,' Andrew agreed.

Georgina knew that any one of these things could threaten Bobby's sight. The burst eyeball, the blood or the rising intraocular pressure. More than one was not a good diagnosis. It would certainly end his budding cricket career.

'He needs to get to Darwin. Now,' said Andrew.

'I'll get in touch with the RFDS,' Georgina said.

'Good. Go,' he said, and watched her depart. 'Can you help me get him over into the shade, Jim?'

Jim nodded and took Bobby's legs while Andrew took his torso and very gently they lifted him off the ground. It was really important now not to do anything that would increase the pressure within the damaged eye and contribute to the raging glaucoma.

Andrew didn't even want to guess what the pressure would have measured had they been able to use a tonometer. The severely swollen eye and closed lid would prevent them from doing so. And ultimately it didn't matter. First aid was the same—cover both eyes and get to hospital. Bobby needed specialist medical care—sophisticated eye testing, X-rays and maybe even surgery.

They placed him in the chair where Georgina had been watching the cricket. Jim left to get some eye pads while Andrew tried to assure Bobby they were getting him some help. He did a quick neuro assessment as best he could through the boy's sobs, satisfied that Bobby didn't appear to have sustained a head injury. The boy's cries had settled to moans and groans and Andrew felt sick, thinking about all the worst-case scenarios. He glanced back over to where Cory was, the elders distracting him from the medical emergency that was unfolding with painting.

Georgina returned slightly breathless. 'A plane will be here in an hour,' he said.

'They landing at Bongaba's strip?' he asked, referring to the outback strip where they had picked up Cory the previous day.

She nodded. Jim returned and thrust some eye pads at them and they worked in tandem, each patching one eye.

'Hey, Doc, nothing wrong with that eye,' Dazza said, who had been hanging around on the fringes.

'I know, but we need to cover the good one as well.'

'Why?' he asked.

'Because what one eye does, the other does, too. If you look to your left with your left eye, what does your right eye do?' Andrew asked, taping the patch in place.

Dazza thought about it and Andrew smiled as he watched the boy experiment with his own eyes. 'It looks to the left as well.'

'Right. So if we cover up his good eye and reduce its visual stimulation, the bad eye won't be trying to work as well and maybe worsen the injury. It's a way of forcing the bad eye to rest.'

Dazza thought about it and nodded.

'Right, let's go. We're going to need to take it slow and steady, so it'll take a while,' Andrew said. 'Can you bring the vehicle over, Jim?'

Jim obliged and Georgina blinked. When had that happened? She was the one who controlled the crises as they occurred out here, as they inevitably did. She gave the orders and took control of the scene. While everyone else ran around like chooks with their heads cut off, she was the one who could be counted on to keep her head firmly on her shoulders. She felt surprised by the power shift but also a little relieved. It was kind of nice to share that burden for once.

Jim parked the car as close to Bobby as possible. They didn't want him to have to exert himself at all and risk increasing his intraocular pressure. Between Jim and Andrew they loaded their patient carefully into the back seat.

'I'll drive,' he said, slamming the door.

'No,' she said, climbing into the driver's seat. 'I know the roads better than you.'

Andrew nodded. She'd made a very good point. 'OK, just take it easy on the bumps.'

As Georgina circled around the main camp, Andrew wound his window down.

'Hey, Cory,' he called out. The group of artists looked up. 'We're going for a drive to meet the flying doc at Bongaba. Do you want to come?'

Cory shook his head vigorously.

'He can stay with us, Doc, we'll keep an eye on him,' Archie said.

Andrew hesitated but then Cory beamed a huge smile at Archie and he knew he couldn't drag him away. That was the smile he'd been waiting six months for—even if he had given it to someone else. Andrew was surprised how much it hurt. Why hadn't he been able to reach him like this? He gave himself a shake—did it really matter? It was a positive sign and he should be grateful.

'That OK by you, Cory?' Andrew asked.

His nephew's face was shuttered again when he looked at his uncle but he was nodding his head

enthusiastically so Andrew put his disappointment aside.

'See you soon, OK?'

'Yeah, see ya,' Cory said, returning to his canvas.

Half an hour stretched into fifty minutes. The
roads were quite rutted and every bump was
agony for poor Bobby. Georgina crawled along
in some places, making the going very slow.
Dazza had asked to accompany them and Andrew
had agreed, thinking they he might be a good
distraction for his friend and to help keep
Bobby's spirits up.

They kept up a constant flow of chatter, Dazza
following his lead well. Andrew was still quite
concerned that Bobby might have a brain injury but
his fear lessened the longer they travelled and
Bobby continued to remain alert and orientated.
The conversation also kept his mind off Cory's
smile—the one that hadn't been for him.

Bobby started to ask some tricky questions
about his sight and Dazza kept looking at him for
answers he didn't have. His best guess was that if
Bobby escaped this incident with no vision loss,
he'd be amazed.

Georgina's gaze met his in the rear-view mirror
on more than one occasion. Her honey eyes were

sympathetic and he knew that she was just as concerned about Bobby as he was.

'How's he doing?' she asked, looking over her shoulder, her teeth worrying her bottom lip.

'He's OK,' Andrew said, injecting confidence into his voice.

'We're nearly there,' she said. The temptation to accelerate was strong, but Georgina knew that slow and steady was what was required of her.

Ten minutes later Georgina pulled the vehicle up near the strip. Like the previous day, Andrew had lost track of the number of convoluted tracks and abandoned paddocks she had traversed. He had no idea how she'd found it, he was just grateful she had.

It wasn't long before they heard the drone of the engine and in ten minutes the RFDS plane had landed efficiently. The door opened, some steps were lowered and an energetic doctor called Helen Young and a nurse called Carl disembarked.

'Oh, nasty,' Helen said, lifting the eye patch to peek at Bobby's injury.

'Yes,' Andrew said, suddenly distracted by Carl's enthusiastic greeting of Georgina. He could see the strapping male nurse out the corner of his eye giving Georgina a very long hug.

Everywhere they'd been in the last week, every male they'd come across had seemed to know her.

The petrol station attendants, the truck drivers, the farmers, the clients. And not just know her. They all seemed to think they could just indiscriminately hug and kiss her. It didn't seem quite fair when he'd been fantasising about a bit of that action himself.

No matter how platonic it was with these other guys, the longer he spent in her company the crazier it made him. He didn't quite understand it—it was wrong and stupid and dangerous to want something that wasn't ever going to go anywhere. But he wasn't feeling very rational at the moment, Cory's smile at Archie still burning in his gut.

'Do you think he's ruptured his globe?' Helen asked.

'Too hard to tell at the moment,' Andrew replied, trying to concentrate on the conversation. 'He'll almost definitely have a hyphaema.'

Georgina laughed and Andrew looked behind him to where she and Carl were standing very close. It shouldn't be irritating him, but it was. He had an eight-year-old nephew and a job in the city. What the hell did he care if she kissed every man in the outback?

In five minutes they had Bobby loaded into the plane and hooked up to a monitor, and Helen was inserting a drip. Carl was assisting, which made Andrew much happier, but when he heard Georgina laugh again he looked out of the aircraft door and saw another man kissing her—the pilot this time. *Hell! Now it was really bothering him. Did the woman know every man in the outback?*

In another ten minutes Georgina had hugged both men again and the plane was taking off.

'He's going to be blind, isn't he?' Dazza asked, his voice cracking as the plane lifted off the ground and they watched it ascend into the wild blue yonder.

Georgina put her arm around the kid and gave him a squeeze. 'We won't know, Dazza. Not for a while.'

'What's a ruptured globe?' he asked.

Andrew looked at Georgina. 'It's where the tissue at the front of your eye tears and lets the jelly stuff behind leak out. Like a burst eyeball,' he said.

'How do they fix it?' he asked.

'There are quite a few surgical options,' Andrew replied, 'depending on the severity.'

Dazza nodded and thought for a moment. 'And what's a hy—hy—what did you call it?'

'Hyphaema,' Andrew confirmed. 'It's a haemorrhage, a bleed, into the front part of the eye.'

Dazza thought again. 'None of them sound too good.'

Andrew and Georgina exchanged looks again. 'No, they're not,' Andrew admitted. 'Both of them can affect Bobby's vision. But we just have to wait and see.'

Georgina gave Dazza's shoulders another squeeze. 'Come on. Let's get back to Tulla,' she said.

Dazza climbed in the back, his shoulders slumped. Andrew climbed in the front with her and they got under way. Georgina's gaze flicked constantly to the rear-view mirror, watching Dazza worriedly.

'So…you're quite the popular girl out here, it seems,' Andrew said quietly.

'Huh?' Georgina asked, her thoughts preoccupied with Dazza.

'Carl and the pilot,' he said shortly.

Georgina looked away from the rear-view mirror and focused on him, trying to fathom what the hell he was on about. 'Carl's parents own a nearby property, we grew up together. He's a mate,' she said. 'Alec has been a pilot with the Royal Flying Doctor Service for ever. He's a good friend of Bomber's. What's this got to do with anything?' she demanded.

'Nothing,' he said. It was as much a surprise to him as it obviously was to her. He was aware that he was being irrational but he didn't seem to be able to stop either.

He was in the middle of nowhere, doing a temp job he loved more than anything he'd done in two years, a withdrawn eight-year-old boy by his side and a woman that every man under one hundred within range got to hug and kiss except him. Everything was making him crazy at the moment. The adrenaline surge over Bobby's crisis had ebbed, leaving him a little strung out, and the smile Cory had given to a comparative stranger replayed in his brain, needling relentlessly.

'I grew up around here. We all know each other. That's the way it is out here, city boy.' She suppressed the urge to poke him in the chest, which was exactly what her fingers were itching to do.

Georgina had no idea why she was getting tense when he wasn't making any sense—but she was. He seemed angry with her for some reason and she wasn't sure why. She'd certainly done nothing to deserve it and she sure as hell wasn't going to accept attitude from a city boy who obviously had no idea how things worked out here. His implication sucked. She could feel her heart pounding in her ears and she braked hard at a gate, the tyres kicking up dust and dirt.

'Georgina,' he said, shooting a hand out to the dashboard to brace himself.

'Damn it, Andrew. The name is George,' she snapped.

They glared at each other across the short

distance that separated them. Andrew could see the heat of anger sparking in the honey depth of her eyes, making them look like melted toffee, and he wondered if her lips would taste sweet like toffee as well. *God, he'd known her for a week and he wanted to kiss her—badly.* He was conscious of the rapid rise and fall of her chest and could hear the occasional catch in her breathing. *He needed to taste her mouth—now!*

But even through the haze of lust that was clouding his vision he was acutely aware of Dazza sitting in the back, looking curiously from one to the other. 'I'll get the gate,' he snapped, and turned away before he was tempted to treat Dazza to a display that shouldn't be witnessed by children.

'What's wrong with him?' Dazza asked, as they both watched Andrew slam the door and storm towards the gate.

'I'm not sure, Dazza. I'm not sure,' she said.

But he'd better snap out of it pronto or he can walk the rest of the way.

CHAPTER SEVEN

ANOTHER two weeks on and they were only two days from moving the service to Byron temporarily. It had taken her a while, longer than she'd hoped, but Georgina had organised a new timetable for the remaining three weeks. The Health Department had issued them with a minibus, which would assist with the transportation of clients from their communities to Byron and back again.

It wasn't the most efficient way to operate but an essential part of the eye service was its flexibility. Things often cropped up out here that would never happen in the city, and Georgina had spent the last five years adapting the programme to fit around such occurrences.

Cory, the reason why they were uprooting themselves to Byron, didn't appear to mind being dragged around the outback. They were in their seventh location since he'd joined them. As long as he had his art stuff, he took the constant packing and unpacking and moving around as passively and submissively as he took everything else.

But Georgina had seen an improvement in him and was encouraged by it, though she knew Andrew still worried. He was eating more and the dark circles that had ringed his eyes a couple of weeks ago were slowly disappearing. He even smiled from time to time. But, still, the road wasn't the place for a child.

Being at Byron would be the best thing for Cory. For one thing, Mabel would make it her mission to fatten him up. But more importantly, it wasn't appropriate to have him constantly around a bunch of adults. OK, he did seem mature beyond his years. She supposed having a blind mother would have forced responsibilities on him that few kids his age would ever have had to think about. But he still needed to socialise with other kids, which he wasn't really doing at any of the camps, preferring to hang out with the elders.

She was keen to introduce him to Charlie. She had a feeling they'd be fast friends. Her nephew, also quite mature for having grown up around a bunch of adults, needed someone his own age, too. And despite their vastly different backgrounds, they both had one thing in common—losing their mothers.

Andrew had taken her advice and was being

more physically affectionate with Cory, too. She knew Andrew was disheartened by Cory's persistent guarded response but she also knew that Andrew was going to have to put in the hard yards with this one if he wanted it to pay dividends.

'Give him time,' she had said to him only the previous day as Cory had passively accepted a hug from Andrew, only to squirm out seconds later.

She had squeezed his hand and smiled at him sympathetically and they had shared a strangely intimate moment that had left her feeling slightly dizzy. Ever since the day they'd come back to Tulla after Bobby, there had been an undercurrent between them that was getting hard to ignore.

She'd decided that strange day to just be polite and stay aloof. But it wasn't so easy to do when she was working with a man she was madly attracted to, despite all the reasons she shouldn't be, and when polite and aloof just weren't her. Georgina was more a tell-it-like-it-is kind of girl. If she liked someone, they knew it. If someone irritated her or riled her, they knew that, too.

She'd wake up each morning vowing to keep herself detached, but over breakfast he'd say something funny or come out of his tent with his shirt unbuttoned and his grouchy need-coffee look and her vow would crumble every time. He made her smile, hell, he made her laugh out loud usually. And he touched something deep inside her, something she didn't want to analyse, with his valiant efforts to reach out to Cory.

He pulled his weight, he didn't expect her to wait on him or have any special allowances made because of Cory. He was kind and gentle with his patients. He didn't pontificate and he didn't patronise. And despite the upheaval in his personal life, he hadn't left. Most of the city guys would have jumped at the excuse to go.

Yet as each day went by he seemed more and more at home out here. A few weeks ago she'd had the impression that he had a lot on his mind and that he'd come here purely as a means to an end. But as time passed she could tell he was really into what they were trying to achieve out here, and he seemed to be embracing it enthusiastically. What if he stayed?

Andrew smiled pleasantly at Georgina as he passed her. She smiled back pleasantly and he thanked his lucky stars he had his sunglasses on and she couldn't see his eyes popping out at her just-out-of-the-shower-attire, which consisted of a towel wrapped around her and nothing else.

Her hair was wet and there were some droplets

that had escaped onto her shoulders. He did not look behind him, just kept on walking to his tent. He calmly unzipped it, threw himself down on the air mattress, pulled his pillow out from under his head, held it over his face and bellowed loudly into the thick cushiony layers.

'Problem?'

Andrew removed the pillow and saw an amused Jim standing at the entry to the tent.

He sighed. 'No. No. Just exercising the old… lungs,' he said, giving his chest a manly slug with his closed fist.

Jim laughed. 'OK. We can play it like that,' he said, retrieving something from his bag and standing again. 'You know where I am if you ever want to talk about George.'

Jim left and Andrew groaned, plonking the pillow back over his head. He removed it after a few minutes and stared at the blue canvas roof of the tent. He could hear the comings and goings of the camp, the low murmuring of voices, the laughter of children, the sound of feet running close by.

This could not be happening! Didn't he have enough to worry about with Cory? He didn't need this bizarre attraction. Georgina was driving him to distraction. She smelt like flowers and had this great bellowing laugh that he found himself listening out for all day. Her clothes were sensible rather than feminine but, ooh, la, la—the way she filled them out was all woman. He was going insane! If he didn't kiss her soon, he would go mad.

But every time he thought about it he thought about all the reasons why starting something with her would be plain wrong. He was leaving and Georgina just wasn't the type you could love and leave. The type he saw in the city. The type who knew the score. The type who appreciated a few dates, a little sex and were happy to leave it at that. The type who didn't want to know and certainly didn't care about an orphaned nephew.

And then there was that look in her eyes. The wary look he saw sometimes when he got up in the morning and their gazes met for the first time of the new day. He'd heard talk around the communities about someone called Joel, and he wondered if that look had anything to do with the mysterious man.

Three weeks. It had only been three weeks and the remaining three stretched ahead of him. Three weeks of sitting next to her while they worked, her perfume blowing towards him on the breeze. Three weeks of watching her sweet-talk Cory. Three weeks of erotic dreams about her. Waking every morning, vowing that each day would be the day he would get a grip and act like a mature adult instead of a horny adolescent. But he just didn't seem to be able to switch his hormones off around her.

At least once they moved to Byron there would be no more catching glimpses of her as she walked from the shower to her tent, her bare shoulders and wet hair tantalising him. No more rubbing shoulders as they prepared breakfast together, sipping at her wonderful coffee. His city *lattès* were never going to match the milky sweetness of her coffee.

Breakfast was fast becoming his favourite time of the day. He would wander outside his tent each morning and she would be standing in the kitchen area, all bright and eager, his coffee in her hands, smiling her good morning smile with those soft pink lips. Very, very distracting lips.

He groaned into the pillow. He didn't need this. He really, really didn't. His life was complicated enough. He didn't need these…feelings. Yes, spending this time in the outback had been good for him. It had been good for Cory, too. But if he'd known that he was going to be creating more problems for himself by coming out here, he would have tried harder to get out of it.

The rumble of the generator cut out and the sudden silence intruded into his thoughts. Now the clinic was over for the day it wasn't required, and Jim had obviously shut it down. Andrew had been surprised at how many of the communities didn't have something as basic as electricity. But, then, he'd learnt a lot and seen a lot out here.

For one thing, he'd never expected it to be so beautiful. Sure, he'd heard that central Australia was a fantastic tourist destination but he'd always preferred more cosmopolitan locations for his holidays. Or exotic resorts. Preferably ones he didn't have to fly to.

He'd known it was big and dry and red but he hadn't been prepared for the utter vibrancy of the colours out here. The sheer beauty of the vastness. And the greenness had totally surprised him. Yes, the wet season had just finished but there was more water than he thought there would be. Any depression in the ground had water in it and the more remote roads were still atrocious in places, potholed and some even washed away.

And for another thing, he'd never expected to love the work this much. The Outback Eye Service was a marvellous teaching environment. He'd seen eye conditions out here that you just never saw in the city. It gave him a new appreciation of the vast divide between outback Australia and those lucky enough to live close to specialised medical services. His determination to raise Cory in the city seemed justified every day when faced with such inequity. He couldn't contemplate bringing Cory up anywhere that was so under-serviced.

He yawned and was tempted to shut his eyes, if only as a pure avoidance measure. All those early mornings must be catching up with him. It had been a pretty full-on three weeks. Not just the travelling but the constant emotional vigilance required to manage the Cory factor as well as his growing attraction to Georgina. He was looking forward to shifting to Byron Downs. And not just for his nephew's sake. Avoiding Georgina should be easier at her family home, in civilised surroundings. Hopefully.

He hauled himself off the bed and felt a lot calmer walking out the tent than he had walking in. He took some deep breaths. He was a thirty-five-year-old man. *A doctor, for crying out loud.* It was ludicrous and beneath him to not be in control of his body. He was a professional!

Georgina chose that moment to exit her tent as well. She was wearing her usual night-time attire of a sarong and a T-shirt. He watched her as she walked over to Megan and Jim and laughed at something Megan said. The edge of the sarong flapped in the gentle breeze and lifted slightly, giving him a brief glimpse of thigh.

He wondered if she slept in it or did she take it off and just sleep in her underwear? Or did she sleep in nothing? The thought of her sleeping in nothing was not a good thought and he looked at Jim miserably before turning around and heading back to his tent.

Georgina looked up from her conversation with Megan and noticed Cory sitting under the shade of a tree, painting as usual, and she wandered over to talk to him as she did most afternoons.

'Hi,' she said.

'Hi.'

He didn't look up. Conversation with Andrew's nephew wasn't easy, Cory's guardedness ever present. But Georgina knew that giving up wasn't the answer. Cory was painting dark brown swirls against a charcoal background. Up in the corner, as in all his paintings, floated a ghostly looking figure in a long white gown with long blonde flowing hair.

She'd not asked him about the figure before. Just praised his work and encouraged him to keep going. To paint out all his sadness and misery. Andrew hadn't pushed him on it either, although she knew he worried about what Cory's paintings actually meant.

Maybe it was time to push a little? 'Who's that?' she asked casually.

He shrugged slim shoulders. 'Nobody.'

She nodded and sat silently, hoping he would elaborate. He looked at her with a searching gaze and she held her breath.

'You have red hair,' he stated.

'Yes.' Georgina smiled and screwed up her nose. 'It runs in the Lewis family.'

Cory nodded and looked back at his painting. 'My mum had blonde hair.'

Georgina grew very still. 'Yes. She was very beautiful.'

He looked back at her. 'So are you.'

Georgina smiled and took his compliment as it was intended, instead of rejecting it, which was always the instinctual thing for her to do. 'Thank you.' *At least eight-year-old boys weren't aware of pear-shaped butts.*

Cory's little hands curled into fists. 'My mum's dead, you know.'

Georgina nodded slowly, not wanting to rush in and scare him off now he obviously trusted her a little. 'Yes, I know. I'm very, very sorry about that, Cory. My mum's dead, too.'

He looked at her sharply. 'Really?'

She nodded. 'Really.'

'Was it a long time ago?' His voice seemed so small for such an adult question.

'Six years.'

'But you're always smiling.'

Georgina nodded again. 'I didn't. Not for ages. I was sad for a long time.'

'I'm going to be sad for a long time, too,' he proclaimed.

'That's OK, mate. You're allowed to be sad. You take as long as you need.'

Cory looked at her with solemn eyes for a few moments then turned back to his painting and recommenced his work.

Andrew ventured out of the tent again and saw Cory and Georgina talking. They looked deep in conversation, their heads close together, her copper spirals a stark contrast to his very fair, very straight fine fluff.

He envied her the ease with which she approached Cory. He was grateful she took the time each afternoon to sit with him and a little jealous of how naturally it seemed to come to her. But, then, dealing with kids seemed to be instinctual with her. She certainly had every child in the communities hooked around her little finger. Was it a female thing?

'What were you two chatting about?' he asked her a few minutes later when she joined him.

Georgina saw the worry in his eyes. 'Being sad, I think.'

'Sad?' *Oh, God. Was that good or bad?*

'He told me Ariel had blonde hair and had died. I think he's starting to open up, Andrew.'

Andrew felt his heart leap. Could Georgina be right? He saw her smile and was encouraged by the hope he could see in her honey gaze. He felt elated, almost giddy with relief, and the urge to kiss her, to thank her with his mouth, was very tempting. A tiny breakthrough with Cory and he had her to thank for it. 'I hope so.'

'You're winning, Andrew,' she said, squeezing his arm.

'Thanks to you,' he said.

She shook her head dismissively, refusing to read too much into his gratitude. She was just doing what she always did, what she was good at—fixing things.

Andrew was chatting to one of his patients a couple of hours later when he felt a tug at his shirt. He looked down to find Cory standing quietly beside him.

'Cory,' he said, smiling at his nephew's earnest face, and crouched down to give him a hug. His nephew had stopped the robotic stance routine but the passive just-enduring-it stance was almost as hard to ignore, and Andrew hugged him a little longer, remembering the old days before his sister's death.

'Have you finished painting for the day, mate?'

Cory nodded solemnly, a canvas by his side. 'I painted something for you,' he said.

Andrew felt his heart bang loudly in his chest. 'Really? That's fantastic, matey. Can I have a look?'

'It's not very good.'

Being at Cory's eye level, he could see the hesitation in his nephew's gaze. But Andrew knew they were taking a big step forward here. Bigger even than the one he had taken with Georgina.

He took a deep breath. 'Your mum used to always say that,' he said keeping his voice light. 'Artists are always really critical of their own work. But your mum was a brilliant painter and I reckon you inherited that from her.'

He watched Cory closely and hoped to God he had said the right thing. Georgina was much better at this than he was. She found it easy to talk to Cory about his mother. It was still a little raw for him, still too fresh.

Cory's face broke into a huge grin that went all the way to his eyes. 'Really?'

Andrew felt as if the sun had come out after months of rain as his heart beat a joyful tattoo in his chest. 'Really,' Andrew said, and hugged Cory again.

Cory broke the embrace as usual, subduing Andrew's elation a little. They still had a long way to go. His little fingers turned the painting around, his face serious again as he presented the painting to his uncle.

Andrew stared at the picture in utter amazement. Larger than life, taking up almost the entire canvas, Georgina's face grinned back at him. Her copper curls spiralled merrily from her head. Her pink lips curved up into an exact replica of her ever present smile. Her freckles blended together to form the precise hue of her skin and Cory had somehow managed to reproduce the colour of her eyes perfectly. More than that, he'd managed to capture the essence of her. It was an amazing piece of art.

'It's George,' Cory said.

'I know…it's incredible, Cory. You are so talented,' Andrew said, unable to take his gaze off the painting. And the best part was that Cory had placed Georgina against a yellow background. Sunflower yellow, like the outback sun. Not black or brown or grey. No ghostly Ariel floating overhead. The whole painting made him happy just looking at it.

He looked at his nephew and Cory was beaming at him again, and Andrew's heart swelled with love and pride.

'What are you two looking at?' Georgina smiled as she approached.

'Cory has painted the most amazing picture,' said Andrew, grinning at his nephew.

'Can I see?' Georgina asked Cory, looking from one to the other, her heart also swelling at the smile bestowed on Andrew by his nephew.

Andrew raised his eyebrows at Cory. Cory nodded and Andrew flipped it around to show Georgina.

Georgina blinked, not at all expecting to see a huge portrait of herself. She looked like she'd overdosed on happy pills. It was fantastic. She smiled and then she laughed and gave Cory a huge hug. She was pleased that this was how he saw her. Hopefully in time he'd realise that you could come out of the other side of tragedy and smile again.

'I love it!' she exclaimed, and kissed his cheek.

Cory blushed. 'Really?'

'Really, Cory. I reckon your mum would be so proud of you.'

Cory beamed at both of them again. 'I need to wash out my brushes,' he said, and skipped away. They watched him go. Andrew glanced at her and smiled. Cory had turned a corner, he just knew it. OK, they still had a way to go, but this was such a promising step.

'Isn't it great?' he said.

Georgina felt his excitement infect her. 'The best,' she admitted.

He looked into her eyes and saw her genuine delight. He knew she'd been instrumental in helping Cory to this point. The thought of leaving and never seeing her again was getting harder and harder. But if this day showed him nothing else, it showed him that he could make a real success of his life with Cory now. And that's what he needed to focus on. His life with Cory. In the city. A million miles from here.

The next morning Andrew's eyes opened suddenly. The face that floated in front of his for those few elusive seconds between sleep and wakefulness was, of course, Georgina's. He could feel the familiar heat in his loins and he made no effort to try and recapture the retreating eroticism of his dream. He'd slept fitfully—thoughts of Cory's progress and images of Georgina chasing each other around his head.

He sat up, his heart pounding loudly in his chest. Cory slept peacefully a metre away, his back to Andrew. It was dark still in the tent and Andrew looked at the luminous dial of his watch. Five-thirty.

As quietly as he could, he pulled on his jeans and shirt he had discarded beside his swag the night before. He exited the tent and zipped it up, wanting to get as far away from his bed as possible. He shook his head to clear the clutter of images and breathed deeply of the early morning air. The very first fingers of dawn reached across the sky, the stars fading almost before his eyes.

For once he was the first one up. Cory wouldn't stir until at least seven o'clock. He started to walk. He needed to expel his pent-up frustration somehow. He knew that Georgina and Cory were incompatible in his life. She belonged here and they belonged in the city and, no matter how many times he turned it around in his head, the solution was always the same.

He walked out of camp and down a path he had seen Georgina take yesterday. He didn't know where it led, it didn't really matter. He was all churned up inside, a walk anywhere would help him sort things out. There was enough light for him to see where he was going so he just put one foot in front of the other and didn't think about it.

It was quite a bushy walk, the tall trees dark ghosts in the gloom. They were in a hilly region and he revelled in the distraction of straining muscles powering up the gradual incline. He could hear the loud chatter of insects and some early birds calling in the new day. The bush smelt sweet and earthy and he breathed deeply, his tension slowly easing.

He became aware of the sound of running water and realised he was following the course of a creek.

Up ahead the track appeared to terminate at an outcrop of rock formations. The sky was almost fully light now so he idly picked his way up the smooth boulders all piled on top of one another. Time and water had eroded holes in the large round rocks until they'd become bowl-like.

The wet season had filled the bowls and they appeared to cascade into one another. Trees and shrubbery grew amongst the rock pools, creating a private haven. It was beautiful and to be here by himself felt very primitive, like he was the only white man to have ever stumbled across them.

He climbed to the very top rock, not a particularly strenuous climb, honoured to sit here in the dawn stillness and be part of this spectacular place. It helped to put his problems in perspective. This place had been here for no doubt millions of years and would no doubt endure a million more. What were his worries compared to the mightiness of this place? A blip in time. Insignificant.

He heard a noise and realised suddenly he wasn't alone as his eyes sought the source of the intrusion into his solitude. *Oh, no!* There, floating on her back at the edge of the rock pool, her eyes closed, her hands acting as rudders, was a barely dressed Georgina. Georgina, who he'd been wanting to kiss for about as long as he'd known her. Georgina, who had helped him find his way back to his nephew. He remembered their shared joy yesterday and felt a surge of emotion in his chest.

She was singing, he realised, and was amazed as her tuneless melody assaulted the air that a thousand birds weren't taking flight. He recognised her favourite song and smiled to himself. She was either wearing a bikini or her underwear. It looked black, whatever it was, and covered what needed to be covered but not enough as far as he was concerned. Her full breasts thrust upwards out from the swirling water, two mounds of ripe flesh taunting him.

His erotic dream returned in full detail and he wondered what it would be like to taste the wet skin along the inner curve of her cleavage. And then wished he hadn't. The rock beneath him had nothing on the hardness between his legs.

Her body had sunk slightly below the level of the water but he could still see the white of her abdomen. Her skin was very pale there and he wondered how his hand would contrast against her creamy flesh. He could see the dip of her belly button and followed the curve of her waist with interest.

Her arms and legs were splayed wide as she circled lazily. Her hair billowed out all around her head, pushed around languidly by the water. He knew it wasn't right to ogle her like this when she didn't know he was here, but she was absolutely gorgeous and he didn't seem to be able to stop. What the hell was she doing here at this hour of the morning? Was this her routine? Did she do it every morning? If he'd known that, he might have been keener to get up earlier.

He watched her for a few more moments than gave himself a shake. *This is voyeuristic, Andrew Montgomery. Leave. Now.* He stood to go, looking back over his shoulder for one last glimpse, and promptly slipped on some loose rock and fell very inelegantly in a loud noisy heap flat on his butt, cursing the entire way down.

Georgina heard the racket and flipped herself onto her tummy then trod water. 'Is somebody there?' she asked the now silent bush.

Andrew got to his feet slowly. 'It's just me,' he said, supporting his back with his hands and testing his ability to walk. Now he felt like a pervert.

Georgina stared at him stupidly for what seemed an age. What the hell was Andrew doing there? Had he been watching her? She blushed. *I'm in my underwear!* She glanced over to the rocky edge a few metres away where her sarong and T-shirt were.

'Have you been here very long?' she asked, trying to be indignant through her embarrassment.

'Long enough,' he admitted. He eased himself gently down the flat boulders until he was standing at the edge of the pool near her clothes. He knelt and dipped his hands into the water to wash the graze where he had put out his hand to break his fall. 'Hell! It's freezing in here,' he said.

Yes, well, I need to cool my feverish imagination down somewhere after a night full of dreaming about you in a damn towel. 'It's invigorating,' she lied.

'It's arctic,' he said.

God, he was gorgeous. His blond wavy hair, his blue eyes, that damn sexy little scar. It didn't seem fair that he was fully clothed when she was practically naked in front of him. 'Oh, go on, city boy. Live a little,' she goaded.

'Right,' he snorted. 'If I want to take an ice bath I'll go to Scandinavia,' he said, standing and examining his hand in a valiant effort to not look at her and her still very visible, barely covered upper half.

'Chicken,' she goaded again, and flapped her arms in the water while making clucking noises.

He chuckled. 'Oh, very mature.'

He was so…dressed. So neat and tidy, and he was looking at her from a superior height and she wanted to see that smile wiped off his face. The same smile he'd given her yesterday, expressing his gratitude over Cory. The one he gave her when she found something he couldn't find or she handed him something before he'd even asked for it.

In such a primitive setting, the cool water stroking seductive fingers across her skin, she'd never felt more like a woman. She was naked, and there was something between them that since yesterday had only been enhanced. She wanted to see the heat she saw smouldering in his eyes sometimes. Despite the futility of their relationship. Maybe it was the water nymph in her, maybe it was the sense that for the moment they were the only two people on earth. She swam around in circles, treading water, flapping and clucking.

He looked down at her. Their gazes met and he saw the challenge in her eyes. She was offering him something straight out of one of his dreams. His heartbeat pounded in his ears. 'If I get into that water, you're fair game,' he warned.

Georgina felt her skin break out in goose-bumps. Her nipples tightened and strained against the fabric of her bra. His voice was low and husky and sexy as hell. 'You have to catch me first,' she goaded.

He saw her honey eyes liquefy to a smooth toffee as she issued her dare. *Right.* He smiled at her triumphantly and before he could second-guess himself he whisked his shirt off over his head. He stopped, his chest heaving, his breath loud in his ears. He raised an eyebrow at her giving the opportunity to call a halt to what was becoming quite a dangerous little game. He could feel his blood rushing through his veins, every cell in his body alive with anticipation. He could feel his mouth watering in the knowledge that very soon her mouth would be under his.

Georgina swallowed and kept her gaze level with his. Did he think she would back down? She could see his naked chest in her peripheral vision, his flat male nipples beaded into tight marbles. 'I don't think you've got it in you, city boy,' she said, her voice husky.

Andrew held her gaze. He unzipped his jeans and shucked his shoes off one at a time, using the opposite foot. He watched as her sure little smile slipped ever so slightly. Then he pushed the denim off his hips, down his legs and stepped out of its confines. His form-fitting underwear did nothing to hide—in fact, barely contained—an erection that not even the thought of jumping into freezing water could dampen. But he looked her straight in the eye and refused to be embarrassed. Country girls needed to learn they shouldn't play with fire.

CHAPTER EIGHT

OH, MY. Georgina's mouth went suddenly dry as she took in all of him. She suddenly understood why women used to swoon. Andrew Montgomery had the whole package. Long legs, great quads and a very large bulge in just the right spot. The water didn't feel so cold any more. Everything felt hot. Very hot.

'Are you sure, Georgina?' he asked, his voice a low, scratchy rumble.

She couldn't back out now, even if she'd wanted to. She knew what was going to happen when he got in the water. And frankly she was tired of fighting it. She'd felt so close to him yesterday that doing this now seemed right. And if she didn't kiss him soon, she was going to go insane.

She gave him a smile and made another chook noise. He reacted instantly and she squealed as he dived into the water straight for her. She kicked away and swam quickly to the opposite side, laughing in sheer exhilaration.

Andrew rose to the surface where she'd been, the

cold water freezing the breath in his lungs. He coughed and spluttered and cursed out loud at the icy fingers of the water. He heard Georgina laugh behind him and he spun around, pushing his hair off his forehead. 'It's a wonder you're not a popsicle by now,' he gasped. He could feel the cold seeping into his muscles.

'Ha, city boy,' she said, splashing some water at him, 'this is nothing. You should try it in winter.'

Andrew chuckled and then lunged for her. She slipped out of his grasp and swam quickly to the other side.

'You know I'm going to catch you eventually,' he warned, breathing heavily, a delightful thrill of anticipation warming him from the inside.

Georgina laughed. 'Of course. That's because I'm going to let you,' she said. 'In the meantime, think of it as a warm-up exercise.'

'Georgina, I've been warmed up for weeks.'

She stared at him for a few moments, breathing hard, thinking about the heat she'd seen so often in his blue, blue eyes. Then he lunged for her again and she laughed and avoided his grasp and they chased each other around the rock pool for ten minutes, splashing and teasing, enjoying the ritual of the chase. And when he finally caught her she didn't protest, but went into his arms very willingly.

Their chests were heaving in unison, their breathing ragged. She could feel his erection against her belly as he supported her in the water, an arm around her waist. Their gazes locked. 'How did you get this scar?' she asked, raising her index finger and touching it. Finally touching it. She'd been too afraid to even ask him about it for fear she'd want to touch it.

'When I was five I wanted to know how Ariel felt, being blind. So I blindfolded myself. Ariel said I was being stupid and that I'd get hurt, but I didn't listen. I tripped over a chair leg and smashed my chin on the glass coffee-table.'

Georgina laughed. 'Ouch.'

'You could say that.' He grinned. 'There was blood everywhere. My mother was yelling. I was screaming. Ariel was hysterical.'

Georgina caressed the smooth broad scar with her finger. 'Poor baby,' she said, and raised her face to lightly kiss it better.

Andrew felt a surge in his loins and knew that with her body so intimately pressed against his she could hardly not have noticed. 'Georgina,' he whispered huskily.

'George,' she whispered back, opening her eyes wide at him.

He chuckled and shook his head, lifting her chin

with two fingers so their gazes could mesh. 'George. Ina,' he repeated. 'You're a woman,' he said, and let his fingers slide from her chin, down her neck and lower still to follow the ripe bulge of a soft breast.

She watched, fascinated by his large fingers against her creamy flesh. Delicious sensations suffused her body and lapped at her internal muscles.

'A beautiful…'

She sensed his mouth moving closer and shifted her gaze to his lips.

'Desirable…'

They inched a fraction closer to her.

'Sexy…'

She could feel his warm breath against her mouth.

'Woman.'

'We shouldn't be doing this,' she whispered.

'I know.'

But then his mouth touched hers gently, briefly, and it was like a tiny spark igniting a drought-ravaged grassy plain. She practically self-combusted. An inferno raged in an instant and she opened her mouth wider, wound her arms around his neck, urging him closer, nearer. Weeks of wanting this so badly erupted into this one kiss.

She was breathing hard and so was he and the

feeling of the kiss quickly raging out of control was igniting spot fires everywhere. Her breasts were aching, her pelvic floor was contracting and deep between her legs an unbearable tingling was causing her to squirm and twist against him.

She flattened her body against his, trying to get nearer, desperate to have every part of her in intimate contact with him. Desperate to ease the ache that had been building inside since the day she'd laid eyes on him. But it didn't help so she locked her legs around his waist, the bulge in his underwear rubbing against her intimately, stoking and satisfying all at once. She felt delirious, desired, sexy. She felt like a woman. Like a George. Ina.

Andrew revelled in the give and take of her mouth, the intimate play of her tongue against his, the pulse in his groin as she rubbed herself against him. It was so much better than it had been in any of his dreams. So much more real. So much more thrilling.

The water seemed like ice against his overheated flesh and as a contrast it was wildly stimulating, but he was finding it technically challenging to tread water, kiss passionately and keep both their heads above water, so he moved her swiftly towards the shallows. Besides, he wanted that top off and he knew he couldn't manage all three things without drowning.

Georgina felt her feet touch bottom and then her back hit solid rock and she found herself lying horizontally, Andrew's weight on top of her on a shallow ledge in the pool.

'Oh,' she said, not even aware that they'd moved.

Andrew grinned. 'Thank Mother Nature. We have our own water bed.' And he kissed her again, hard.

Georgina moaned against his lips and opened her mouth again, but he pulled away. 'Oh, no, you don't, no more distractions. This is next,' he said, pointing to her bra and then drawing a circle around her nipple on the outside and smiling triumphantly when he felt the bud harden beneath the fabric. 'I want to taste you,' he said.

Georgina felt the slam of desire tighten her internal muscles. She saw the heat and smouldering intent in his gaze and remembered how many times she had dreamed about him making love to her. She reached for the front clasp and whipped the black scrap of lace away.

Andrew watched as her breasts sprang free, buoyant in the water, the nipples tightly scrunched. He sucked in his breath. 'I wanted to do that,' he half complained, trying to decide where he wanted to start or whether he just wanted to look at their magnificence for a little while longer.

'What's the matter? Don't those fancy city girls

take the initiative?' she teased huskily, incredibly turned on by his blatant appreciation.

He chuckled and looked at her for a moment then quickly sucked a nipple deep into the warm cavern of his mouth. He smiled at her harsh indrawn breath and revelled in her deep appreciative moan. 'You were saying?' he asked, lifting his mouth temporarily to look into her lust-drunk eyes.

'I…um…' she said, not sure of her place in the conversation any more. And when he sucked her other nipple, grazing his teeth lightly against the sensitive tip, she didn't even try to keep up.

Then, suddenly, noisy laughter nearby shattered their intimacy. Andrew broke off his ministrations abruptly and protectively covered her near-naked body with his own.

'It's down in the lower pools,' she whispered into his neck, assuring him as much as herself as she tried to get control of her tripping heart and ragged breathing.

He nodded, the intrusion bringing with it an inevitable dose of reality. She shifted out from under him and he moved, too. She sat on the ledge and drew her knees up to cover her nakedness. He sat beside her.

'Now, that's what you call a bucket of cold water,' she said.

He chuckled. 'We've been making out in a bucket of cold water—it doesn't seem to have mattered.'

They sat silently for a few moments. 'We'd better get back,' she said, a sudden chill making her shiver. 'I think my bra is a goner.'

'No, look, there it is,' he said, and pointed to the scrap of fabric floating in the middle of the rock pool, the cups keeping it buoyant.

Georgina laughed. It looked so forlorn, bobbing around in the middle of nowhere.

'I'll get it,' he said, and pushed away from the edge.

Georgina took the opportunity to get out of the pool. She really didn't want to, suddenly self-conscious again about her body and her state of undress. It seemed absurd, given what they'd been doing only minutes ago, but she wasn't sure how she was supposed to act now. She wrapped her sarong around her shoulders.

'Here,' he said, vaulting out of the pool.

She watched helplessly, unable to stop. His arm muscles rippled and the water sluiced off his chest and flat stomach and, despite the intimacy now being completely dead, he still had a most impressive erection. He handed her the bra, seemingly unembarrassed or unashamed of his near nudity or his state of arousal.

'Thanks,' she said, taking it from him, their fingers brushing, the energy between them still there despite the noises of kids swimming below.

He turned to get into his clothes and she took the opportunity to hastily throw hers on, too. They walked back together in relative silence, lost in their own thoughts. Georgina knew she should be cross at herself for letting it happen, but truthfully it had been too good to lament. It had been a long time since she'd been kissed so thoroughly and she seriously doubted if she'd ever been kissed that well.

Andrew was just too blown away to be able to fully analyse all the pros and cons. It certainly complicated his life. And it was definitely complicated enough. But maybe this had been a healthy outlet for something that had been fairly inevitable right from the beginning? Maybe they could go about their work now minus the undercurrent that hummed between them?

'How come you were up so early?' Georgina asked, breaking into his rationalising.

'Dreams,' he said, smiling down at her. 'You?'

'Same,' she said, blushing hard as his knowing chuckle feathered her skin with goose-bumps.

They headed straight for their tents when they re-entered the camp. Most people were up and about by this time and if they wondered why Georgina and Andrew were emerging from the bush rather damp at such an early hour, nobody asked. Andrew was grinning as he opened his tent zipper, suppressing an insane urge to whistle.

It died quickly as he heard Cory's anguished sobs. 'Cory, what's wrong?' he asked, throwing himself down beside his nephew. Cory was curled up in a ball, his arms clutched across his abdomen, and he was rocking himself.

Georgina peeked her head into the tent, having heard Andrew's worried exclamation.

'Have you got a pain?' Andrew asked, trying to pry the boy's arms away from his stomach so he could investigate.

'You were gone,' Cory cried. 'I woke up and you were gone, just like Mummy.'

Andrew felt his earlier happiness sink like a stone. He glanced at Georgina, their earlier experience tarnished by a sudden jolt of guilt. His nephew had been lying there, crying, while he'd been making out with Georgina? No, no no. He looked at Georgina hopelessly.

'I was just with Georgina, Cory. I didn't think you'd be awake for a long time. I'm never going to leave you, mate.'

He placed a comforting hand on his nephew's

shoulder which Cory promptly shrugged off. Andrew closed his eyes castigating himself for his stupidity. What must Cory have gone through when he'd woken to find his uncle had disappeared? They'd been so close yesterday, closer than they'd been since Ariel's death and now Cory looked as distant as he ever did.

Georgina could see the regret written all over Andrew's face and couldn't bear that she had been the cause. It was funny how something so wonderful could be viewed in such a different light at another time. She'd known they were impossible but something like this really emphasized the gap between them.

She watched Andrew lie down beside his nephew and pull his little body in close. His big arm encircled the boy's waist and although Cory held himself rigid, Andrew tucked him in close anyway. She backed out of the tent as Andrew rubbed his chin against Cory's hair and dropped a kiss on his head. Uncle and nephew, together. A team. A unit. A family.

She heard him say, 'I'm right here, mate, I'm not going anywhere,' as she zipped the tent up. Andrew was stepping up to the plate. He'd come a long way in a few weeks, too.

But her arms ached and her womb ached and her heart ached, knowing their actions had caused a child such distress. A child who had already been through too much already. She shook her head in disbelief. How could they have allowed their own needs to take precedence over Cory's?

Andrew's attention span was shot for the rest of the day. Between worrying about Cory and thinking about Georgina and the rock pool, he was really distracted. And it was a bad day to be easily distracted. He was operating and performing surgery on an eye was very delicate, requiring intense concentration.

Georgina wandering back and forth, her floral perfume wafting towards him, usually at the most inopportune time, not helping this process. Visions of her topless in the water, her nipple in his mouth, warred with visions of Cory awake and upset, the memory of his anguished cries tearing at Andrew's gut.

How could something so amazing suddenly be so sullied? He shouldn't have lost focus. Things with Cory were still so precarious—he couldn't afford to take his eyes off the ball again. Cory had to be his priority.

Georgina, too, was distracted as she assisted Andrew with the surgery. It was obvious from his aloofness that Andrew blamed himself for Cory's state of mind that morning, and after being so intimate earlier it seemed odd for them to be so distant, so detached.

She tried to maintain a professional distance but scrubbing in with him required a degree of closeness in the cramped confines of the caravan. Their shoulders rubbed, their fingers brushed as she passed him instruments, their gazes locked above their masks, and, despite the futility of it, the fire in her belly grew hotter.

Trying to keep a distance seemed strange now when all her feminine instincts that he'd so successfully roused were telling her the opposite. She wanted to lean into him. Get closer. Nearer. Smell him. Taste him. Bat her eyelids at him. Flirt.

Flirt? Where the hell had that come from? She didn't flirt. She'd never flirted. Even with Joel she hadn't. And there were more important things at stake here. Like a damaged eight-year-old boy. She was letting her imagination make more out of the rock pool than there had been. Whatever had happened there had soon been overshadowed.

The little fantasy bubble they'd been in for those brief moments of ecstasy had burst dramatically and their lives had been brought back into sharp focus. He had commitments and responsibilities and a life far from here, and she had Byron and the eye service—there was no room in her life for any more city boys.

They broke for lunch and Georgina was relived to be out of such close confines. She ate her sandwich, acutely aware of Andrew and Cory sitting nearby, eating theirs. She admired Andrew's fortitude. He kept up a constant stream of chat, trying to bring Cory back out of the shell he'd retreated into. She eavesdropped unashamedly.

'I've been thinking, Cory,' Andrew said, 'about your painting of Georgina. How about when we get home we frame it and hang it in the lounge room so we can always remember our time out here?'

Andrew almost sank to his knees in thanks when Cory stopped chewing, stopped staring morosely at the ground and looked him square in the face.

'Really? You really think it's good enough to hang on a wall?'

Andrew could sense Cory contemplating his first tentative step forward. He nodded enthusiastically to draw him out and felt like he was finally reconnecting with his nephew after that morning's debacle.

'Absolutely. Don't you think so, Georgina?' he asked, looking around for her support.

Georgina looked up from her food, nodded and

smiled. 'I reckon it's good enough to hang in an art gallery,' she enthused.

Cory looked at her and then at his uncle and a slow smile spread across his face. The boy suddenly looked a foot taller.

'That'd be neat,' he said. 'When we get home.'

Georgina was thankful that uncle and nephew were too engrossed in each other to see the smile fade from her eyes. Home. Back to the city. Back to their lives. And she would continue on here with hers. The rock pool this morning and sharing yesterday's breakthrough and this morning's crisis with Andrew had been so intimate it was easy to forget she wasn't part of their equation. Easy to forget that she didn't want to be.

She finished her lunch listening to a more animated Cory and then busied herself with cleaning up and preparing for the afternoon theatre cases.

'Thanks.' Andrew's low voice warmed her ear. 'You seem to always know just the right thing to say.'

'No probs,' she said, not glancing up from the very important job of washing the dishes.

He watched her fussing around in the sudsy water. 'About the rock pool,' he said. Had it been only that morning? It seemed like such a long time ago now.

No, not that. She'd been trying to forget the rock

pool all day. It had been a mistake. 'It's OK. I think we should just forget it happened,' she said.

He looked at her and could see the vulnerability not quite hidden in the depths of her honey gaze.

'Can you do that?' he asked quietly.

Georgina tossed the knives and forks a little too forcefully into the wire drainer. 'We're not teenagers, Andrew,' she said impatiently, wanting this conversation to be over.

He moved his mouth closer to her ear. 'When I'm old and grey and my brain is addled by Alzheimer's, I hope the rock pool is the one thing I don't forget.'

His voice was low and husky and she clutched the plastic bowl as its timbre stroked across her pelvic floor, causing a quiver deep inside.

He cleared his throat. 'I wish my life was different, less complicated. I'm sorry… This is really bad timing…'

'It's OK, Andrew.' She sighed. 'You have your priorities and I have mine. That's just the way the cookie crumbles.'

And she picked up a towel and began to dry.

Georgina woke the next morning at her usual time with an image of Andrew disappearing as quickly as a desert mirage. She rolled on her side and curled herself into a ball, her thighs squeezed together tight, trying to relieve the ache that a head full of rock-pool dreams had put there.

She hugged herself. What the hell was she doing? She should know better than this. Had her experience with Joel taught her nothing? Getting involved with another city boy was just plain madness. They were worlds apart. And not just in distance. He was used to neon lights and shopping malls and the ballet. And there was nothing like that out here.

But they had things that were just as good. Better.

They had campfires and night skies to die for. They had Bomber and his mail run, bringing exciting packages from mail-order catalogues. And they had bush dances and coroborees and the mystical rhythm of nature as it ebbed and flowed in its ancient dance.

She got up and walked outside, the approaching dawn still and perfect. Her feet were bare and she revelled in the feel of the soil. This dirt was in her blood, the call of the land resonating in every cell.

There was a bond she couldn't explain. It was completely intangible. Fine, like the silk strands of a spider's web—delicate but resilient, too. Her family lived here. Her mother was buried in the rich red earth here. And she belonged here also.

And no amount of charm and bright city lights could sway her again.

She had everything she needed here. A job and family and friends. She had money and food and a beautiful old house to live in. She could see. She had her health. She was free to come and go. She was much better off than so many people. People needed and depended on her, and it gave her purpose.

Then why did it suddenly feel like it wasn't enough? Why wasn't her heart singing like it usually did at this hour of the morning as she counted her blessings? Why had a city doctor suddenly made her feel like she wanted more?

A dog barked and she shook herself out of her reverie. She'd better get cracking. They had all their post-ops to see and then they had to pack up camp and travel the five hundred kilometres to Byron. She could feel the stir in her blood again. She was going home.

When the vehicles pulled up at the homestead, Georgina felt her heart swell with love and pride to see her family waiting on the steps to greet the convoy. Good old-fashioned country hospitality demanded no less. She realised as she looked at them through the dusty window that everything that was important to her was right there. Her father and John and Charlie and Mabel and even the newly discharged prof all waving and smiling down at her.

She glanced at Andrew, who was helping Cory gather his stuff. He had his family. His commitments. She looked back at Charlie and smiled as he waved his arms enthusiastically. This was what was important. Her family. Her commitment.

Charlie rushed forward to meet them, followed more sedately by the others. Georgina grinned at her nephew as she pushed open the door and gratefully set her feet on Byron soil. She absorbed the impact of his eager hug, sweeping him into her arms.

'George, George, is he here?' he asked eagerly.

Georgina had told Charlie on the phone a week ago that she was bringing him a playmate, and he'd apparently not stopped talking about it ever since. Having a child his age around to play with was a true novelty.

She laughed. 'Yes, Charlie. Steady on, you'll frighten him off.'

'Hello Georgie girl,' said the prof, pecking her on the cheek.

Georgina couldn't believe how well her boss looked, compared to the last time she had seen him. She had been worried deep down that she may never see him again, but he looked like he had years left in him. The prof had obviously been really run down—they needed to find a replacement fast.

'Harry, you look fantastic. I'm so pleased you're going to spend some time relaxing with us at Byron.'

He chuckled, the rasp in his voice back in full force. 'Mabel wouldn't have it any other way.'

'You better believe it, Harry James, you old goat.' Mabel laughed as she embraced Georgina.

The prof had removed a cataract from Mabel's left eye ten years ago and she was his number-one fan. Mabel would fuss over the prof and see he ate well.

Andrew came up behind Georgina and shook Harry's hand. 'Great to see you looking better, Prof.'

'Fit as a Mallee bull,' he said, thumping his chest. 'I'll be right as rain when your rotation is up.'

Georgina opened her mouth to protest but Mabel beat her to it.

'We'll see, Harry James. We'll see.'

Andrew chuckled at the prof's insulted look, conscious of Cory sticking close to his side. The welcoming party was noisy, with people and talking and hugging and kissing in one big press of bodies.

He noticed Charlie eyeing Cory and could see

Georgina's nephew's patience running out. 'Hi, Charlie,' Andrew said. 'This is Cory.'

Charlie, who had been displaced by the crush of bodies, moved closer and stuck out his hand. 'Hi.'

Cory regarded the gesture seriously for a moment and a hush fell over the group. Two eight-year-old boys. Two complete opposites. A freckled redhead and a pale blond. A country boy and a city kid. All the adults were clued into the situation and they all waited with bated breath.

Cory stuck out his hand, too. 'Hi.'

They shook hands firmly and the adults relaxed a little.

'You have red hair,' Cory said, dropping his hand, 'like George.'

'Yeah. I got it from my dad. This is my dad,' Charlie said, gesturing to John.

Cory waved. He was silent for a few moments and then said, 'Where's your mum?'

Everyone held their breath again.

Charlie shrugged. 'She's dead.'

More silent contemplation. 'So's mine.'

'What happened to yours?' Charlie asked.

Andrew felt himself tense.

'She got run over. What about you?'

'Plane crash,' Charlie said.

The two eight-year-olds nodded solemnly at each

other for a few moments, for all the world like two adults shooting the breeze over cattle prices or the stock market.

'You wanna see my horse? You can ride him if you like,' said Charlie.

Cory shook his head. 'Can I paint it?'

Charlie thought about it for a moment and shrugged. 'OK.'

'How about I take you two in for a snack first?' said Mabel.

'Cool,' said Charlie, and took Mabel's outstretched hand.

Mabel held her hand out to Cory and smiled her gentle smile. Cory took it and followed them into the house.

'Well, I'll be damned,' said Andrew, amazed at Cory's immediate acceptance of both Charlie and the older woman. 'She always have this affect on kids?' he asked Georgina.

'Yup,' she said, smiling at the housekeeper's obvious pleasure. Mabel hadn't been able to have her own kids, which had been such shame. Kids absolutely loved her.

'Right, who's for a drink?' said Edmund, rubbing his hands together and grinning at everyone broadly.

There was a resounding murmur of agreement.

After three weeks in 'dry' communities, the thought of a cold beer was mighty inviting.

They moved inside and Georgina showed Andrew where he'd be sleeping. He followed her through several rooms and down a long wood-panelled hallway. It was dark and cool and with all the evidence of a hundred years' worth of add-ons, a bit like a rabbit's warren.

'Where should we put Cory?' Georgina asked, as Andrew threw his bag on the bed. 'Charlie is keen to have him share his bedroom but I told him we'd have to wait and see.'

Andrew nodded and sat on the bed gingerly, testing the springs. A real bed. With a real mattress. Luxury. Not that he had minded sleeping rough— on the contrary, he'd been pleasantly surprised— but it made him appreciate the mod cons even more. Andrew glanced up at her, her honey gaze making him acutely aware that they were in the presence of a very big bed.

'I'll ask him later this evening and see what he wants to do.'

She nodded, staring at the bed, memories of Andrew kissing her in the rock pool returning unbidden. 'Right, well…come out and join us for some drinks when you're ready,' she said, leaving before she heard a reply, escaping quickly down the hallway and trying not to think about him sleeping under her roof.

It was ridiculous really. They'd slept in closer proximity the last few weeks than they would be now, but sleeping in the tent next door didn't seem as intimate somehow. This was her home she was sharing with him, her family. And after he was gone there would be memories here of him not just in this room but all over, and she already knew he was going to be hard enough to forget.

CHAPTER NINE

THE next two weeks flew by for Andrew. Every few days Jim and Megan would pull into Byron with a minibus full of patients to be examined and treated. To make allowances for the travel time, they sped up their routine a little. Instead of taking a day for the examinations and the next to operate, they examined in the morning and operated in the afternoon.

It was a little more rushed than normal but nobody seemed to mind. The clinic started earlier and finished later and there wasn't as much time for impromptu cricket, but the smiles when the eye pads came off the next day were still as broad. The thanks were just as genuine. Andrew sometimes felt if that smile, that joy could be made into a pill, no one would ever be depressed again.

Edmund and John had erected enough tents in Byron's yard to accommodate everyone and Mabel—who had once been a shearer's cook—coped with the extra mouths to feed like a pro. The next morning the post-op checks were carried out and then the patients would get back on the bus and be taken home.

By far the most common thing Andrew continued to see were cataracts in his older patients and conjunctivitis in the young. Although he had also removed quite a few pterygiums, which was something he'd rarely seen in the city. Of course the close link between this eye condition and exposure to direct sunlight was, no doubt, responsible for the disproportional number of cases.

The raised, wedge-shaped growths of the conjunctiva were usually more irritating than dangerous. Most remained dormant, causing only redness and tearing, but he'd seen quite a few out here that had grown over the central cornea, affecting vision, and Andrew had had no choice but to surgically remove them so the patients could see.

There was a lot of the run-of-the-mill stuff, too, that Georgina picked up through testing visual acuity, usually with the children. Long-sightedness, short-sightedness and astigmatism. But diabetic retinopathy was also common. A significant portion of their adult patients had type-two diabetes and had suffered vision loss due to the tiny blood vessels of the retina becoming weak and haemorrhaging.

There wasn't a lot Andrew could do for the vision

already lost, but he referred all the cases he saw to Darwin to undergo preventative laser therapy to protect their remaining vision. Andrew would have loved to have had the equipment there to do it and had even worked out the logistics in his head, but he understood more and more as he watched Georgina juggle the finances that services such as these ran on the whiff of an oily rag and under the constant pressure of reduced funding.

And then there was Cory. The difference in him in two weeks was astounding. Much to Andrew's relief, Charlie and him had become good friends. It seemed their shared bond of being motherless had united them, despite their differences.

Sure, Cory was still the quieter of the two, content to follow rather than lead, but Andrew could see him coming more and more out of his shell each day. He laughed more, he talked more, he ate more. He painted less and when he did they were like the Georgina portrait. Colourful, very similar to the boldness of colour his mother had always preferred.

And funnily enough Mabel had become his new muse. Cory, when not with Charlie, could be found with Mabel, painting her doing whatever she was doing. Knitting or cooking or dozing in a squatter's chair on the verandah. He seemed to have developed a real bond with her. From the moment she'd held out her hand to him that first day, she'd become his adopted grandmother or something.

Andrew suspected that Cory was drawn to her calmness. Charlie was an energetic country kid who was always on the go, and Cory seemed to enjoy that a lot, but underneath it all he was still a little boy grieving for his mother so Mabel's quiet serenity, her unobtrusive manner, her whole-hearted acceptance of him was soothing to Cory's broken heart.

In fact, from time to time Andrew was a little jealous of the easy connection his nephew had with Mabel. Glad of it in so many ways and so grateful to Mabel for taking the time with Cory, but a small part of him wished it was him.

He was still waiting for Cory to return his hugs. Or, better still, to spontaneously initiate one, like he'd done when Uncle Andy had come to visit. Those days seemed so long ago now. The days when he would be walking out the door with Cory clinging to his leg like an oyster on a rock, begging him for one more cuddle. Andrew secretly despaired that that day would ever come again.

But he tried not to dwell on that too much and concentrated on the positives. Cory had done things out here he would never have done in

Sydney. He'd scattered grain for chooks and collected their eggs and bottle-fed potty claves and hung around with jackeroos. The prof had showed the boys through the caravan and told them gory eye-op stories. And Cory had even sat with Charlie while he'd done his school of the air every morning.

When they went back to Sydney in a week's time, Cory would have a wealth of experiences that his city friends would never have. And so would he, for that matter. And they both had Georgina to thank for that.

Georgina. He watched her sway over to Megan and smiled as her rich laughter drifted towards him. He thought about the day she had laughed and teased him at the rock pool. He could still remember the taste of her mouth, the coolness of her skin. He dreamt about it every night and woke each morning with a smile on his face and a frustrating ache in his groin.

Fortunately he could still remember what had happened afterwards and his guilt over that morning persisted. It had certainly put a natural halt on things and being busier now and her having her family around all helped. Still, he couldn't believe he had survived another two weeks in her company without dying of lust. Because despite the guilt there was something between them that was hard to ignore, and he knew she felt it, too. But the situation was hopeless and his life was complicated enough and that, as she had said, was just the way the cookie crumbled.

Georgina could feel Andrew's gaze on her, even though she was talking to Megan. She actually wasn't concentrating particularly well on what her friend was saying, but Megan didn't seem to be aware. The hairs at her nape prickled as she felt the weight of his continued stare. Hell, she was going insane! If she had one more rock-pool dream she was going to scream.

She had almost knocked on his door at two a.m. the previous night, prepared to completely debase herself and beg him to finish what he'd started. She could barely concentrate these days because of him. OK, starting a relationship would be a bad thing. Since the rock pool Andrew had been painstakingly platonic. Cory was his priority and she expected nothing less.

But she occasionally saw a flare of heat in his eyes that scorched her insides to charcoal and no amount of Joel memories could put out the fire. She was beginning to wonder if it was possible to live with this much frustration without dying. Would having a fling with him be such a bad thing?

OK, one-night stands weren't her thing, but she was nothing if not adaptable. Living out here, you adapted or you perished. And she'd never been one to hide from a problem—that just wasn't the country way. She should do what she always did with any dilemma that crossed her path. Tackle it head on. She knew what she needed to make it go away. She just didn't know how to ask for it and was wary of the potential long-term side effects.

The Joel experience had left scars. Maybe they weren't on the outside, like Andrew's sexy little number, but they were there none the less. OK, she'd known Andrew long enough to know that he was no Joel. But did that really matter when ultimately Andrew would leave her for the city as well? She needed to stop wasting her time falling into old patterns and find herself a nice country boy.

But in the meantime the ache in her breasts and her belly and between her legs gnawed away at her. When he brushed against her, her nipples hardened. When he laughed, her pelvic floor muscles quivered. When he stared at her, like he was now, her heartbeat trebled. Could she really watch him walk away in a week and not know at least one night's pleasure in his arms?

The war raged within her as Megan chatted away.

The satellite phone rang and she answered it thankful for some respite from her rampant hormones. It was Peggy, and after some pleasantries Georgina took a deep breath and took the phone to Andrew.

Their gazes locked as she ambled over and she could feel her eyes growing hot from his stare. He made her feel so female when he looked at her like that. She had to suppress the instinct to thrust out her chest and exaggerate the sway of her hips. *Oh, God, get a grip!*

He was sitting on the edge of the verandah at the top of the four wide steps that led into the homestead entrance. His perfectly muscled legs, bare from mid-thigh down, were bent at the knee, each foot resting on a lower step. His blond hairs on his arms and legs were a perfect foil to his light tan. He looked for all the world like he belonged there. In the outback. In her home.

Their gazes drew level and she spent a moment totally lost in the possibilities she saw in his stare.

'Peggy,' she said, handing him the phone.

Andrew took the phone, noting the way her fingers lingered slightly. 'Hello,' he said, refusing to drop his gaze from hers.

Georgina couldn't have moved even if she'd wanted to. Listening to his voice was an erotic experience in itself and she was too damn weak to move away. And then there was the way he continued to stare at her as he murmured into the phone. Her tongue flicked out to moisten her lips because she was suddenly so parched and she noticed the flare in his eyes.

'Wendell's been sentenced to five years jail for art fraud,' Peggy said. 'It was just on the news.'

Now, that got his attention! He broke eye contact with Georgina. 'What?' Andrew demanded.

Peggy filled him in and Andrew listened intently. Much to his shame, he actually hadn't given Wendell a lot of thought since Cory had come. His nephew was safe with him and Wendell was just one of the many things he was going to have to deal with when he got back to Sydney. But this news made the Wendell issue redundant and elation thrummed through his body.

He rang off and grinned at Georgina. He vaulted down the stairs, grabbed her face between his hands and kissed her hard. It was giddy and foolish and he didn't care. Then he picked her up and spun her around, letting out a loud whoop.

'What? Put me down.' She laughed.

He slid her down his body and kissed her again. 'Wendell's been a naughty boy. He's going to be a guest of Her Majesty for quite a few years.'

Georgina's head reeled from the delicious passion of his kiss. Her heart banged in her ears and she was breathing hard. *Oh, to hell with it. She wanted him.*

She took a deep breath and threw caution to the wind. 'Why don't I take you for that campout under the stars tonight that I promised you ages ago?'

Georgina's suggestion was so unexpected it wiped the grin off his face completely and brought his delirious mind back into sharp focus. He looked down into her pretty freckled face, trying to read her honey eyes. She smiled at him, a frank, open smile, and he saw what he was looking for. She knew that if they went out there tonight, things would change for ever.

'I'd like that,' he said.

By five o'clock they were just about ready to head out in the tray back utility. It wouldn't be dark for another couple of hours and Georgina knew it would give them time to get where she wanted to go and get set up for the night.

Cory had been remarkably nonchalant about Andrew spending the night away. Andrew had worried about it and he and Georgina had been totally prepared to sacrifice their night under the stars if his nephew had seemed at all distressed by the thought. Memories of what had happened that morning after the rock pool were still vivid and Cory had come too far for Andrew to willingly do anything to impede his progress now. But it was a real measure of Cory's improvement that he had given his permission without a backward glance.

Mabel thrust a wicker basket packed with food at them.

'We're only going overnight,' Georgina chided, as she took the basket and almost dropped it because of its unexpected weight.

The older woman shrugged. 'Can't have our guests going hungry.'

Georgina laughed and gave Mabel a quick hug.

'Thanks, Mabel,' Andrew said, smiling at the motherly, grey-haired woman.

Georgina packed the food in the car and Mabel put a stilling hand on his arm. 'Be careful of our girl,' she said quietly.

He looked into her creased face; her blue eyes stared unwaveringly back. There was no hostility. Her gaze was friendly but her concern was evident. 'I will.' He nodded.

She smiled at him and removed her hand. Georgina's dad and brother pulled up in a cloud of dust just as they were getting into the car.

'Heading out?' Edmund asked, as he gave his daughter a big bear hug.

'Yep. Gotta show the city boy what true camping out is.'

He picked up Mabel's basket out of the back. 'Oh, yeah, that's really roughing it.' He chuckled. Edmund turned to Andrew and winked. He stuck out his hand. 'Take good care of my little girl, Andy.'

Edmund's hand hold went on a little longer than was necessary and Andrew got the message written clearly in the man's steady gaze. It was almost comical. He'd never met another woman who needed less taking care of. But Andrew knew that wasn't what Georgina's father meant.

'Dad!' Georgina said, rolling her eyes. 'I'm a hell of a lot more capable of taking care of myself out here than Andrew.'

'That's not what I meant,' Edmund said, as he let Andrew's hand go but continued to hold his gaze steadily.

Georgina looked from Andrew to her father and then at her brother, who was also regarding Andrew seriously. She felt her face grow hot and shook her head. 'I'm thirty-one years old, for crying out loud. Come on.' She dragged Andrew by the sleeve. 'Let's go.'

'Sorry 'bout that,' Georgina said, as she accelerated away, wheels spinning.

Andrew chuckled. 'It's OK.' He respected it, actually. 'They're just looking out for you.' Like he'd once looked out for Ariel.

Georgina stopped at their first gate, turned to him and said, 'I know what I'm doing.'

Andrew blinked at her direct gaze. A frisson of anticipation tightened his abdominal muscles. He swallowed. 'I'll get the gate.'

He got back in the car and refused to think about the night ahead. He didn't want to strategise it or analyse it. He just wanted to enjoy it and let whatever was going to happen happen. And hang the consequences.

'I haven't been this way before, have I?' he asked, as they passed through undulating country, generously treed.

Georgina laughed and shook her head. 'You city boys, I don't know. No sense of direction. No, we're heading towards the creek that lies across the southern boundary,' she said.

'And do you have a specific location in mind or are we just going to drive until we find a spot we like?'

She smiled at him. 'I know a place. It's my favourite spot. It's…special.'

She looked so beautiful, her hair loose around

her face, her soft pink lips curved up, her honey gaze sweet and flirty. She was taking him to her favourite spot. 'Just like you,' he said, and stroked the back of his hand down her cheek.

She drove for about forty-five minutes, her heart tripping along at what the night would hold, the anticipation building into a delicious thrill inside. The sun was starting its descent when she pulled the ute up under one of the many river gums that lined the fertile banks of Byron Creek.

'Fancy a dip?' He grinned at her, rock-pool images abounding as they exited the car and he took in the beauty of the water at sunset.

Georgina laughed. 'Sure, if you want to be croc food, go right ahead,' she teased.

'There are crocodiles?' He looked at the pretty setting with new eyes.

She nodded. 'Big ones.'

'Right. No swimming.'

She rolled her eyes. 'Come on, city boy, help me collect some kindling for the fire.'

He followed her lead, picking up twigs, sticks, bark and dry leaves, which were plentiful in the area. He helped her unload the bigger pieces of firewood from the back of the ute. He threw them on the ground where she was crouching about ten metres away from the vehicle and back from the creek bank.

'Wouldn't it be better to set up camp under a shady tree? The sun will be right in our faces in the morning.' He knelt beside her and passed her logs as she indicated them. 'Or is that too close to the bank for comfort?'

'Nah, it's not about the crocs. Two things,' she said, holding up two fingers. 'One, the trees will block our view of the sky and, two, they don't call gumtrees widow-makers out here for no reason. The incidence of campers being killed or seriously injured by falling branches is a little too high for my liking.'

Andrew was beginning to think it was more dangerous out in the middle of nowhere than in the city. He laughed. 'Crocodiles. Falling branches. Anything else I should be aware of?'

Georgina smiled at him. God, he was so beautiful. *Just my heart.* 'Nah. Stick with me, city boy, you'll be fine.'

Andrew smiled down at her. 'I intend to.'

She felt her pelvic floor muscles spasm and her gaze lingered for a little longer before she dragged it away and concentrated on the fire. At this rate she wasn't going to need a match. She'd be able to light the damn thing just from the amount of heat she was generating.

'Do you want me to light it?' he asked, as he

watched her fingers fumble with one and then another match.

She looked at him with doubtful eyes. 'Thanks, I've got it.'

'Hey.' He chuckled. 'I may be a city slicker but I do know how to light a fire. I was a Scout.'

She burst out laughing, trying to imagine him dib, dib dibbing. 'Right, but they didn't teach you about croc habitats or gumtrees?' She laughed again and her heart skipped a beat when he laughed with her. 'If you want to be useful, grab the swags and Mabel's basket out of the car, will you?' she asked when her laughter died.

'Lucky for you I don't have ego issues.'

She sobered a little at his playful words as he moved away. He didn't. Joel had been very sensitive to her teasing about his lack of he-man, bush skills. So much so that she had stopped very quickly. Andrew took it all in his stride with a quick laugh and deflected it with a snappy, witty reply. Her city-boy tag didn't seem to threaten his masculinity or his sense of self. It was nice to be so unguarded.

She struck her third match, relieved to see it ignite. She was all fingers and thumbs with him around, his arm brushing hers, his voice rumbling low and sexy in her ear. She may as well have been born in one of those fancy city mansions for all the skill she was showing lighting the fire.

She held the lit match to the kindling and coaxed it along by blowing gently on the smouldering leaves. A flame sprang up and she began to add more fuel bit by bit.

'Well, let's see what Mabel packed us,' Andrew said checking her out as he approached. She was leaning forward, her chest on her folded knees close to the fire, her denim-clad butt round and cute and tempting.

He unfolded a swag and laid it about a metre from the fire and sat on it, opening the lid of the basket. 'Ooh, tablecloth, red check, very classy,' he said, pulling it off the top. 'Hmm. Nice cheese. Some crusty bread. Ah…' He pulled out a bottle of white wine that had been stashed in a cooler bag. 'Very nice,' he said, holding it up for her to see.

Georgina sat back on her haunches, having built the fire up nicely. It was about twenty minutes to sunset, the sky now glowing with vibrant reds and golds like a stained-glass window. She joined Andrew on the swag, satisfied with her work.

'Two glasses,' he said, handing them to her.

'Corkscrew?'

He slapped one into her open hand. 'Scalpel,' he

said, and laughed as Georgina giggled at his medical joke.

'What else?' she said, as she worked on the cork.

'Some sausages and eggs…for breakfast, I suppose. And some stuff in a container…' He opened the lid. 'Looks like spaghetti Bolognese,' he said. 'It smells good, whatever it is.'

'Everything Mabel cooks is good,' she said, the cork slipping out with a resounding pop.

'A bag of marshmallows and some chocolaty stuff,' he said, opening the corner of another container.

'That'll be Mabel's famous home-made rum and raisin chocolate bar.'

Andrew could smell the chocolate aroma wafting towards him and could feel his mouth water. 'Sounds wonderful,' he said.

'Oh, you have no idea,' she groaned. 'It's my one true weakness.' She handed him a glass of wine.

He took it. 'What shall we drink to?' he asked.

She hesitated. 'How about to good food?'

No. 'How about to weaknesses?'

His voice slid over her like warm chocolate and she shivered despite the proximity of the fire. She raised her glass and touched it to his. The wine was cold and dry with a hint of wood and she sighed as she savoured the crisp taste. Could this moment be any more perfect? A crackling campfire, an outback sunset, great wine and a gorgeous man.

'So, what's so special about this place? I mean, it's very beautiful, apart from the crocs and falling branches.' He grinned. 'But I got the impression it had particular significance for you.'

She nodded. 'It does… There's a place not far from here…I'll show you in the morning.' Of course, by the morning it would be so much more special.

He sipped his wine. 'Do you come here often?' he asked.

'Not as much as I'd like,' she said, helping herself to some Camembert and bread.

'Well, I feel honoured that you've brought me here.'

'You'd better be.' She smiled, the firelight warming his face as the last light of day slipped from the sky and the velvet-blue twilight encroached. 'I've never brought anyone here.'

Andrew swallowed the mouthful of creamy soft cheese, regarding her seriously. The orange fingers of firelight accentuated her copper curls and glowed in her honey eyes. 'Not even Joel?' he asked.

Georgina stopped chewing.

Oh, way to go, idiot. A look of something, maybe wariness, had crept into her eyes and he hoped he hadn't ruined the mood. 'I've heard him mentioned a couple of times.' He shrugged.

Georgina wasn't surprised that Andrew seemed to know about her ex-fiancé. Just because she didn't talk about him, it didn't mean she could prevent anyone else from gossiping about him. But the significance of his words was slowly dawning on her. She hadn't brought Joel here. Why? Had she been afraid he wouldn't appreciate it? Or that he would sneer, like he always had? And why had she been so sure that Andrew wouldn't?

'No. I didn't bring him here.'

Andrew wondered if he should attach too much significance to the fact that she had brought him. 'Oh?'

'Joel didn't appreciate the bush very much,' she said, choosing her words carefully.

Joel sounded like a bloody idiot. Even a city slicker like him could more than appreciate the beauty out here. Sure, he loved the hustle and bustle of Sydney but he also loved the quietness, the starkness, the anonymity out here. 'Preferred the bright lights, huh?'

She smiled. 'Something like that.'

Andrew knew everyone out here compared him to Joel. He knew that Mabel's and Edmund's warnings had been because of Joel. If he was going to be judged, it was only fair to find out as much as he could. 'So what happened? Did he break your heart?'

She sighed. It was such a nice evening. She didn't want to spoil it by rekindling old memories. 'I don't really want to talk about it,' she said.

Her honey gaze begged him to understand. He reached out a hand and pulled gently on a spiral curl brushing her forehead. 'Georgina, something's happening between us. We mightn't like it. It might not be wise. But it is happening. You've been holding me at bay because of him. I need to understand why.'

Georgina drew in a deep breath. He was right, of course. 'It was a whirlwind romance.' Her voice sounded shaky so she cleared her throat. 'I met him in Darwin. We were engaged two months later. He was so...everything. Gorgeous and funny and smart and witty. I felt like such a hick beside him sometimes. And all the single women in the hospital wanted him. But he chose me.'

She looked at him for understanding. And he smiled and nodded for her to continue. 'And then Jen died and I came home for a bit. He didn't seem to mind. But when my mother got cancer soon after it was a different story. It was devastating, especially on top of Jen's death—we hadn't recovered from that yet. So I came home to help out and to nurse Mum. And Joel...didn't like it. He wanted me by his side. He never really got my attachment to Byron. So I spent six months going back and forth to Darwin and we argued a lot and the last month before she died I couldn't get there at all. I couldn't leave my mother...didn't want to leave her. And...'

Georgina remembered how he'd rung every day, asking her when she was coming back. She'd been so in need of someone to lean on. Her father and John had been like lost souls. Her brother had just buried his wife and could barely cope with breathing, let alone a dying mother and a needy one-year-old. She had been exhausted from propping them up and taking care of her mother and Charlie. She'd been so tired of being the brave one. She'd needed Joel's support, his understanding. And he'd failed.

'He didn't even make it to Byron for the funeral, and I knew that day that it was over.' She looked away from him, embarrassed to feel tears threatening. Surprisingly not tears over Joel. She didn't feel hurt or angry any more, talking about him. But reliving those awful weeks before her mother's passing still hurt like hell.

Andrew caught the shimmer of tears. *What a jerk!* He placed a finger under her chin and turned her face back to him. 'I'm so sorry about Jen and your mother—that must have been really hard.'

Georgina nodded, tears completely blurring her vision, spilling down her cheeks. *Why hadn't Joel been able to say that?* That's all she had needed. An acknowledgment of her grief.

Andrew's innate understanding paved the way for her to tell the complete story. 'There's more,' she said, swiping at the tears, displacing his hand. 'I had a miscarriage a week after we buried my mother. I didn't even know I was pregnant. I think I was so run down by everything. The pill was ineffective. It was such a shock.'

Andrew blinked. His memory threw up every child she'd nursed, every baby she'd soothed, every intimate connection she'd ever made with Cory. And he understood suddenly why she was so good with kids. How devastating must losing a baby have been to a woman who thrived on making children happy? He felt her disbelief, her devastation.

Poor Georgina—she'd been through so much. 'Did you tell him?'

She shook her head. 'Never.' She felt a sob rise in her throat and Andrew hauled her into his lap. She laid her head against his chest. The tears flowed. She cried for her sister-in-law and her mother but mostly for her child, who'd never had a chance to live. All the tears she hadn't been able to cry because her father and John and Charlie had needed her to be the strong one, even through the completely unexpected loss of her baby.

Andrew rocked her gently and waited patiently for the tears to dry up.

'I'm sorry,' she said, wiping her face a few minutes later. 'I don't know what came over me. I never cry.'

He chuckled. 'I think maybe that's half the problem. You know it is OK to cry, right?'

She smiled at him through watery eyes. His white scar was emphasised by the firelight. 'Not out here it isn't. Dissolving into girly tears has never been much of an option, growing up around a bunch of men. The jackeroos still tell stories about the day I fell off my horse and broke my arm and didn't shed a single tear.'

He rubbed his face in her hair, his chin resting on top of her head. 'Well, even tough guys like you need to cry every now and then. If you ever need a discreet shoulder to cry on, I'm your man.'

Fat lot of good that's going to do me when you're gone. They sat quietly for a few more minutes then Georgina roused herself out of his lap. 'Let's heat up Mabel's spag bog,' she said, 'can you pour some more wine?'

They laughed and joked as they prepared their dinner, talking about work, sticking to safe subjects. Their voices sounded loud in the vast empty space and it was so primitive that Andrew had the now familiar sensation of them being the only two people on earth at the dawn of time.

Georgina was right. Mabel's food was delicious. And the company was fabulous and the firelight was romantic and the stars were incredible. Andrew had eaten at five-star restaurants on Sydney Harbour that didn't have remotely the same ambience or quality of food.

He finished his bowl and used some bread to mop up the remaining sauce. Not something you could do at a five-star restaurant on Sydney Harbour. Then he lay back on the swag, looking up into the night sky. Myriad stars twinkled like a mirror ball. 'Do you know much about astronomy?'

Georgina put her empty bowl down and reclined next to him. He wriggled over a little to give her some room. 'Not really,' she said, licking her fingers and trying to act like she lay next to gorgeous men every night in the middle of nowhere. 'Bomber's the expert. I just know the basics.'

She was soft and warm beside him and her floral perfume teased his senses. 'There's the Southern

Cross,' he said, pointing to the five-star constellation low in the sky.

He was warm and solid beside her. She could smell his earthy male scent. She laughed. 'Very good, city boy.'

'Hey, I know my Australian icons.'

Georgina pointed out a few more stars that she knew. It was beautiful, gazing up into the inky blackness, Andrew by her side. Her full stomach, the slight buzz from the wine, his low rumbling voice and his sexy laugh made her want to curl into him and purr.

He chose that moment to turn to her, their faces level, and smiled. '"She walks in beauty, like the night. Of cloudless climes and starry skies; and all that's best of dark and bright meet in her aspect and her eyes—"'

Georgina smiled and took over. '"Thus mellowed to that tender light which heaven to gaudy day denies."'

'You are a romantic,' he accused with a grin.

'It's my favourite poem,' she admitted. 'Do you know the rest?' she asked.

'"One shade the more, one ray the less…"'

Georgina laughed. 'OK, OK, I believe you.' She couldn't bear to hear him recite it, knowing in a week he would be gone. 'Let's eat chocolate and toast marshmallows,' she suggested, springing up.

Really, she shouldn't eat chocolate because it would go straight to her butt, but her heart was suddenly heavy and Mabel's home-made chocolate goodies always made things better. It was like a rub and a kiss from your mother when you'd injured yourself as a child—worked every time.

Andrew savoured the clash of flavours. The bitterness of the dark chocolate, the crunch of the nuts, the plumpness of the rum-soaked raisins. And he savoured Georgina's appreciation. Her sigh and moan of pleasure as she devoured the treat was very distracting.

'Here,' she said, passing him a longish thin stick. 'Let's go all out.' And she opened the pack of marshmallows and put one on the end of his stick.

There followed an in-depth conversation about toasting techniques. He was a gently-heat-not-too-close-to-the-flame toaster, she was a flambé-it-til-it's-crispy toaster.

'See, taste this,' she said, blowing the flaming marshmallow out and gingerly pulling it off the stick. She thrust it towards him, the heat burning her fingers.

Andrew leaned forward and opened his mouth. Georgina forgot all about her singed digits. The thought of feeding him the hot sticky sweet caused an erotic fizz of pleasure down low. He stared at her, his gaze challenging her, and she pushed the crispy offering into the warm cavern of his mouth.

Her breath caught as his lips closed over her fingers. The small burn to the pad of her fingers tingled as his tongue soothed the sting. Their gazes locked. He took his time, removing the last vestiges of marshmallow from her fingers, his tongue circling suggestively, before he slowly withdrew his mouth.

'Mmm. Not bad.' Andrew could feel his body responding to the glow of desire in her eyes. He heard her uneven breath and felt a jolt in his groin. 'But this is better,' he said, and turned away from her to toast his own with a trembling hand.

Georgina watched dazed as he slowly hand-rotisseried the white marshmallow. She could still feel his tongue swirling around her fingers. She glanced at his profile, his scar close to her. The desire to touch it was overwhelming. She wanted to run her finger over it, feel its smooth, flat surface as she had that day at the rock pool.

'Now this,' he said, squeezing the marshmallow lightly, satisfied with its internal consistency, 'is perfect.' He slowly removed it from the stick and turned to face her. 'Open your mouth,' he said huskily.

She obeyed and held her breath and his hot stare as he inched his offering closer. Her nostrils flared as the sweet sticky aroma drifted closer, her mouth watered, her hand trembled. She felt it nudge her lips and almost moaned out loud as he slipped it into her mouth. The centre oozed into her mouth, and the hard jut of his index finger tasted divine as she mimicked his movements and slowly sucked his finger clean of the sticky sweet.

Andrew slowly withdrew his finger. She had some marshmallow residue on the corner of her mouth and his gaze zeroed in on the temptation.

'What?' she whispered, as she watched his pupils flare.

'You have…oh, it doesn't matter,' he said, cupping the back of her head, his mouth swooping to remove it.

He kissed the corner of her mouth, his tongue lapping at the marshmallow crumb, gently dissolving it with erotic strokes. He heard her moan and withdrew, catching his breath, gauging if her need was as great as his. Her eyes looked like warm honey and her lips tasted like marshmallow and she wanted him. He could see it in her eyes. In the little mew she made when he'd stopped kissing her.

'We probably shouldn't do this,' he said huskily, gently brushing some curls off her forehead. 'It'll complicate things.'

'I know,' she said, and leaned forward, brushing her lips lightly against his.

'I can't stay,' he said.

'I know. And I won't leave.'

'I know.' She looked so desirable in the firelight. He wanted to see all of her. Feel all of her. Be deep inside her. 'But if I don't make love to you, I'm going to go crazy,' he whispered.

'So let's just have tonight,' she said, smiling up into his face, and claimed his lips in a deep, passionate kiss.

Her lips were hot and sweet, just as he had fantasised. He backed her down to the ground and she went eagerly, clinging to him, her hands clutching the back of his shirt, kneading his shoulder blades. She moaned and opened her mouth wider for him and he felt his heart trip as he pressed against her body, totally lost in the wonder of her mouth.

Her hands moved down his back and he felt each muscle ripple in anticipation. She squeezed his bottom and his erection surged against the constraints of his fly. She slipped her hands beneath his waistband, her skin hot against his bare buttock. He groaned into her mouth, thrusting his tongue inside, wanting every part of him to be closer, nearer, deeper.

'George,' he cried, dragging his mouth from hers.

She looked up at him, missing him already. 'Oh, now you call me George.' She smiled.

'I want to see you. I want to see all of you,' he said, and lowered his mouth to hers again, plundering its sweet depths, their tongues meshing in an ancient dance.

Georgina broke off. She struggled to half sit with his weight pressing her into the ground. She raised herself onto her elbows and whipped her T-shirt off over her head quickly, catching his lips again instantly, unable to bear being parted from them for any length of time.

He kissed her some more and she felt like she was drowning, and when his fingers found her lace-covered breast and stroked lightly across it, teasing the nipple, she realised there were worse ways to die. His hands found the front clasp and her breasts sprang free and she felt the cool air hit them before his hot mouth obliterated everything else.

He lifted his head and looked into her eyes. 'You're beautiful,' he whispered.

Right now, his mouth worshipping her body, she believed him. Her freckles and her pear-shaped butt and her curly mop of hair didn't exist in this universe. Just Andrew and his mouth and his voice and his kisses. He made her feel beautiful. She tried to focus on his compliment but his mouth laved the other nipple and she lost all rational thought.

And then he started to move lower, and all higher functions were totally lost. She felt totally basic. Like the true biological organism that she was. Fulfilling her basic function. Out here with only the stars as their witness, it was almost primal. She felt like a cavewoman, pleasuring her man, and it felt right.

Somehow he'd made short work of her cargos and suddenly she was totally naked in front of him. His tongue traced a trail from her belly button down to her tingling centre.

'No,' she cried out, her hand on his head. If he went there she wouldn't be able to think. 'Not fair. I want to see you also. All of you.'

He looked up her body and caught her gaze. He could see the slight rise of her tummy and the dip of her belly button and the slope of her ribs and the thrust of her breasts and he wanted to know every inch of her.

He chuckled and kissed her belly, releasing her. He rose to his feet and quickly removed his clothes until he was standing above her, completely naked, his erection standing thick and proud.

'Oh, my.' She smiled up at him. The glow from the fire bathed his naked body in soft light. The planes and angles softened, the muscles smoothed. He looked like he'd stepped out of a nude painting. He was perfect. And he very obviously wanted her.

'You do this to me,' he said huskily.

Georgina sat up, stroked her hand down his thigh lightly covered in blond hairs. Felt the muscles there twitch and relax. Her head was almost level with his jutting manhood. She reached for it tentatively. Heard his swift indrawn breath as she traced her finger around the head and then down the length of the shaft.

'Georgina,' he groaned.

She saw the naked desire in his gaze. 'I want you inside me,' she whispered. 'Now.'

Andrew didn't need to be asked twice. He dropped to his knees and eased her gently backwards to the ground. He covered her body with his, plundering her mouth as his hardness found her softness. He slowly sheathed himself in her warm, soft centre and swallowed her moan as she dug her nails into his back.

'Oh, God,' she whispered. 'Again.'

And he did. Again and again. She clung to him and panted and begged and urged and he could feel her body tremble as her orgasm built. Her moans were driving him wild. She was so responsive, so sensitive to his every movement. Her cries were driving him to fever pitch. He could feel the tension in his loins and savoured the slow exquisite build-up.

Georgina felt the niggle wearing away at her resistance. She knew the wave was coming but didn't want it to break. She wanted to kiss him more, she wanted to feel him pounding into her more. If they only had tonight she didn't want this moment to end. But the more he pounded, the bigger the niggle, until she was trying to hold the entire ocean back.

And when he grazed his teeth against her neck it couldn't be held back any more. And it broke. 'Andrew,' she cried, clinging to his shoulders as he pounded faster and faster. Her orgasm jolted through her and her body bucked and writhed beneath him. She heard him cry out and felt him come with her, and she opened her eyes.

The sight before her brought new meaning to the expression about seeing stars. A kaleidoscope of lights danced in front of her eyes. It was like the heavens had provided her with her own personal firework display as the pleasure popped and fizzed through her veins and undulated through every muscle.

Andrew's heart pounded as his orgasm released. He held on to her tightly as she cried out and trembled, and knowing that they had reached nirvana together seemed right in such a primal setting. He felt like they were Adam and Eve in the Garden of Eden. The only two people on earth.

He lay on top of her for what seemed an age, regaining his breath. She moved under him and he rolled onto his back, gathering her close. The stars winked at him as if to say your secret is safe with us.

'I think I'm falling in love with you,' he said into the deep outback silence. It was something that he could say only at this moment. It was rhetorical and futile but the stars and his pounding heart demanded no less than the absolute truth.

Georgina glanced up at him and smiled. For tonight she would take his admission at face value and be grateful she'd heard those words at all. Anything, even their no-win relationship, seemed possible in the afterglow of their love-making, under the magic of a million outback stars.

CHAPTER TEN

'WHERE are you going?' Andrew growled, not even bothering to open his eyes, grabbing her hip, dragging her back to him.

Georgina lay in the circle of his arms, spooned against him, and sighed contentedly. 'It's time to get up,' she said.

He cracked open an eyelid. The sky was just starting to glow a very faint orange. 'It's barely daylight,' he murmured into her neck. It may still be too early for his fuzzy mind but parts of his body were already well and truly awake.

'It's the time I always get up,' she said, feeling her skin break out in goose-bumps at the barest brush of his lips against her skin.

'So? It's Sunday. Is there somewhere we have to be?' His hand lazily stroked the curve of her hip and the dip of her waist.

His voice rumbled low in her ear and the erotic scratch of his whiskers were making her wish they never had to be anywhere ever again except here, in each other's arms. 'No. But you know us country girls, up with the birds.'

He chuckled. 'Even the birds aren't up yet.'

She smiled and felt the clench of her stomach muscles as his finger trailed higher. 'It's a body-clock thing.'

'Well, reset it,' he said. 'We've only had three hours' sleep.'

Georgina blushed, thinking about how insatiable they'd been. The pleasure had rolled on deep into the night. Neither willing to stop. As if touching each other was a biological imperative. They had gone on until they'd collapsed from exhaustion. 'And whose fault is that?' she asked.

'Yours,' he growled, biting her neck gently as his hand cupped a breast, his thumb stroking a nipple.

Georgina felt her eyes close as a surge of desire coursed through her body. She pushed back into him involuntarily, his erection pressing against her cheeks. She wiggled her hips a little until it was nudging her entry. She heard his swift intake of breath and smiled.

'Let me introduce you to the pleasures of sleeping in,' he said, squeezing the fullness in his hand as he surged up into her in a quick, decisive stroke. 'I've got just the right sleeping tablet.'

She gasped. His hardness felt so good. The angle

was incredible, putting pressure on points she'd never known existed. 'I think I'm pleasured out,' she said, and lost her breath and her train of thought as he withdrew. 'I don't think it's possible.'

He chuckled into her neck, his hand leaving her breast and traveling south, finding his target as he surged into her again.

'Oh…God,' she whispered.

Dawn broke as their cries rose to a crescendo. A flock of cockatoos scattered in startled flight as Georgina screamed out Andrew's name. She fell into an abyss where nothing but he and her and all-consuming pleasure existed. And as they landed gently before the rushing ground came up to meet them, Georgina fell into the promised slumber in a wonderful post-coital haze, Andrew still buried to the hilt inside her.

The sun was higher in the sky and the day properly under way when she woke the next time.

'Wake up, sleepyhead,' Georgina said, rolling herself on top of him, kissing the flat white scar on his jaw and then laying her head against his chest, listening to the deep, even thud of his heartbeat.

He smiled, her springy copper curls tickling his chin, and put his arms around her, caressing her bare back. He felt her skin roughen as goose-bumps spread across the area he was touching. 'What time is it?' he asked.

She heard his voice vibrate through his chest. 'About eight o'clock,' she said. She kissed his mouth quickly and managed to evade his hand long enough to get herself out of the zipped-up swag.

Andrew looked up at her standing before him, laughing. She was completely naked. 'Come back,' he said.

'No.' She laughed. 'Get up.' Georgina looked around and collected her scattered clothing piece by piece. Conscious of his gaze following her every movement, she picked his shirt up and threw it at his head.

'Hey, I was enjoying the view.' He grinned, pulling his shirt off his face.

'I know,' she said, and walked away, her clothes bundled in her arms.

He watched her head towards the car, her naked butt swaying, her hair bouncing. She turned slightly and looked over her shoulder at him and he caught the curves of her breast and hip, the twist of her body emphasising the smallness of her waist. He watched her until she disappeared behind the vehicle. How could he go back to the city without her?

No. No. No. Get up. Get dressed. Don't think

about it. Don't spoil the memory with thoughts of the future. He rose and put his clothes on, inhaling the morning air, nothing but red dirt and trees and scrub as far as the eye could see. He poked at the not quite dead fire with his discarded marshmallow stick and memories from last night flooded back.

He smiled as he crouched and resurrected the fire from the pile of kindling they'd collected the previous day. By the time Georgina rejoined him, the fire was well alight.

'Not bad for a city boy,' she teased as she fished around in the basket for the sausages and eggs.

He laughed. 'Well, I'll take that as a compliment.'

They cooked breakfast together and laughed and joked and chatted, an intimacy to their every move. Andrew didn't want to go back to Byron. He didn't want to give this up.

'Come back with me,' he said.

Georgina stopped chewing and looked at him. He was serious, his blue gaze unwavering. Her heart leapt even as her head knew it would never work. 'Come on,' she said, standing up, ignoring his words. 'Let's pack up. I want to show you something.'

He stared after her as she busied herself. *OK, she may take some convincing.* He rose and helped her and together they made short work of it. After three weeks with her on the road, he could pack up a campsite with the best of them. They threw the billy water on the fire and kicked dirt over to be sure it was fully extinguished.

'Where are we going?' he asked, as he climbed into the vehicle next to her.

'Wait and see.' She smiled.

They travelled for about five minutes, Georgina trying not to focus on his declaration of almost love last night and his breakfast proposal. It would be an impossible relationship and she hoped that pretty soon he'd understand why. She saw a large patch of wildflowers and pulled up abruptly.

'Wait here,' she said.

'What are you doing?' he called after her as she exited the car.

She was back in the car a minute later, thrusting a hastily constructed posy of little yellow and purple flowers at him. 'Hold these,' she said.

They drove another five minutes and joined the main dirt road that linked all Byron's paddocks. Two minutes later they were crossing the creek over a rickety-looking bridge and following the watercourse west. Another minute and Georgina pulled the car up under the shade of a tree.

'Come on,' she said, grabbing the flowers from him.

He got out and followed her. He could see a low iron fence up ahead. It was square, a bit like an animal enclosure from a distance, and as they drew nearer he could see headstones. It was a cemetery, far enough back from the creek to not endanger it during the wet season but close enough to hear the occasional trickle of water. Some old ghost gums bordered it, the branches hanging down low, providing a shady little spot.

The gate creaked as Georgina opened it and Andrew stood outside and watched her as she distributed the flowers between three graves. He waited in silence for her to pay her respects and held out his arm to her when she was done, and she went eagerly into his embrace.

'Jen's? Your mother's?' he asked.

She nodded and they stood side by side, arms around each other's waists and silently watched the graves. There were about twenty headstones. Andrew's gaze scanned the inscriptions. There were a lot of Lewises. There were even some Lewis pet graves.

'Who's Floyd Granger?' he asked, looking at the other grave she had decorated with the tiny flowers.

'Mabel's husband,' she said.

Andrew noted that he'd been dead for twenty years. 'What happened to him?'

'A snake spooked his horse during a muster and it threw him. He broke his neck. He died instantly.' Georgina still remembered her grim-faced father returning early from that muster.

They stood for a few more minutes. A gentle breeze rustled through the leaves overhead.

'It's nice here,' he said.

She nodded. 'The aboriginals believe that burial ground is sacred. This ground is sacred to me.'

Andrew knew they were talking about more than just a set of graves. 'I can see why,' he said carefully. 'There's a lot of history here. A lot of heritage.'

She nodded. 'Yes, there is. This is my ancestral home.'

Andrew was hearing the subtext loud and clear. 'Isn't home where the heart is?' he asked.

'My heart is here,' she countered, kicking at the ground with her dusty boots. 'Its dirt runs through my veins. I was born at the homestead. My mother is buried here.'

Andrew felt his heartbeat slow and boom in his chest. 'I'm not asking you to leave and never come back,' he said quietly.

'I stood here six years ago while they put my mother in the ground and I swore on her grave that I would never leave Byron again.'

'Not even for love?' he asked.

She snorted and broke away from him, wandering a few feet away, her back to him, her head spinning. 'Especially not for that.'

'I'm not Joel,' he said quietly.

She sighed and turned to face him. 'I know that. I've known that for ages and if I hadn't I certainly would have known it last night. Joel would never have stayed overnight in anything less than five stars.'

Fool. 'Why settle for five when you can have five billion?' He shrugged.

She gave a weak laugh. 'You could have that every night. If you didn't go back…'

He looked at her. She was beautiful. And she was asking him to stay. 'I…have to…'

'Because of Cory?'

'Yes. And Ariel.' His eyes begged her to understand. 'I promised her I'd make a difference.'

'You are making a difference…out here.'

'With ROP.'

'You were five, Andrew. You think Ariel would want you to do something you're not happy with?' she asked gently. Georgina may not have known Andrew's sister but she did know that John would never want *her* to do something for him that she didn't want to do.

'Of course she wouldn't. But it's more complicated than that. I'm the one who hogged all the room in the womb and inhibited her growth. I'm the one who came out bawling and was home from hospital two days later. I'm the one who could see. I'm the one who's still alive. I know it's not rational but I have to try and make amends for that. She was my twin. It gets me here,' he said, clenching a fist over his heart.

Georgina could see how deeply his guilt ran. And he was right, it didn't sound rational, but, then, human feelings often weren't. He would rather pass up a chance at a new life for him and Cory than betray a thirty-year-old commitment to his sister.

'You love this job, I know you do. How long has it been since you had this kind of job satisfaction in Sydney? Life's too short, Andrew.'

He strode towards her, feeling almost suffocated by the gap between them. He wanted last night back. There had been no gap last night. He stopped before her and gently pushed a curl out of her eye. 'You don't know what you're asking me. You're asking me to give up everything that's important to me.'

She felt the warmth of his palm as he cupped her cheek and laid her hand against his. 'But it's OK for you to ask me?'

'I think I'm a little more anchored then you are.'

She shut her eyes and bit back a scream, answering much more calmly than she felt. 'Yeah…Joel never got it either.'

Andrew dropped his hand and cursed himself, dragging her against him. He'd just dismissed everything she'd been trying to tell him by showing him the graveyard. 'I'm sorry, that was a stupid thing to say. I know the ties that bind don't always have to be tangible.'

She felt better for his apology. She knew he was kicking himself for his statement. She relaxed in his arms and leaned into his strength. Despite everything, all the reasons why she shouldn't, she had fallen in love with him.

'OK, so that won't work. We'll compromise. We'll commute,' he said, easing back a little from the embrace.

Georgina felt her heart sink. A long-distance relationship. She'd been down that track before. OK, it had been a giddy, fanciful relationship, not remotely grounded in the reality of their situations and with one of them nowhere near as committed to it, but its damage had stayed with her for a very long time.

She looked into his face. He was so convinced. 'It won't work,' she said quietly.

'It will if we make it work,' he said eagerly.

'Travelling here and back from Sydney is two

days in itself, Andrew. And you can't drag Cory backwards and forwards all the time. Which would mean I would have to commute and I've been there and done that before. It will wear thin really quickly. Then we'll argue. And the whole relationship will become about what we can't do, can't have, instead of what we do. You'll start to resent it. Then you'll start to resent me.'

'Don't say that. I could never resent you,' he said, cupping her face in his hands. 'That thing I said last night? I don't just think it, I know it. I love you, Georgina. Please, help me work this out.'

Georgina felt hot tears well in her eyes. Here in the place she loved more than anything on earth, she'd heard the words every woman wanted to hear. If it hadn't been so impossible, it would have been perfect. She covered his hands with her own. 'For what it's worth, I love you, too.'

She gently pried his hands off her face and eased away from him, walking over to the iron fence, her mother's grave blurring before her eyes. 'But I won't do the city-country thing again, Andrew. I know you have commitments that you can't break and I wouldn't ask you to because I know they make you the wonderful, compassionate man that you are, and I love you for it. But I'm committed here, too. Not just to Byron but to my family and the prof and continuing the service that he started. Don't ask me to give them up.'

God, this couldn't be happening. She loved him, too? 'What are we going to do?' he asked miserably.

She shrugged. 'Get through this week and then chalk it up to experience. Be adults. You go back to your commitments and I'll stay here with mine.'

'This really sucks,' he said.

She nodded. 'Yes. It does.'

He walked towards her and stood behind her, placing a hand on her shoulder. Just being this near to her was enough to make him want her. 'You really love me?' he asked.

'Really,' she said, turning in his arms, standing on tiptoe to give his mouth a slow, bitter-sweet kiss.

'I don't want to never be able to do that again,' he said, his voice rough with longing, his thumb rubbing along her bottom lip, which was moist from his kiss.

She sighed and slumped her forehead against his chest. They had to stop this. It wasn't getting them anywhere. *Get a grip, Georgie girl!*

She roused herself. 'Come on. We have to get back.'

He let her go and they walked silently back to the vehicle. Two of the most miserable in love people in existence.

* * *

Later that afternoon, Andrew was sitting on the front verandah in a squatter's chair, feigning interest in some medical journals he'd brought with him. They had some interesting articles on the latest ROP research, and he desperately needed to reconnect with his commitment to the cause.

Georgina was with Mabel and the boys, who were picking vegetables from the garden. Edmund was out on farm business and John was tinkering with something in one of the machinery sheds. The prof was dozing in front of the television.

It was an idyllic outback afternoon. Until Charlie came screaming up the stairs.

'Cory's been bitten by a snake,' Charlie said to Andrew, his eight-year-old voice shrill and shaky.

Charlie's terrified announcement slammed into him. Fear clawed at his gut. He felt as if the whole world had stopped turning. Like his heart had stopped beating. Cory? No.

'Where?' Andrew asked, his voice calm despite the maelstrom of emotions lashing his insides.

'In the garden,' he said.

'Go wake the prof,' he said to Charlie, squeezing his shoulders firmly, trying not to panic the boy who already looked distressed enough. 'Tell him to bring the first-aid kit.'

He watched a wide-eyed Charlie go and then he sprinted down the stairs, trying to be calm and think like a doctor, not a terrified uncle who'd already failed his nephew too many times. *Dear God, please, let him be OK.* The thought that he had put Cory at risk to satisfy his own career needs was too much to bear after all they'd been through.

Andrew ran. He could see Georgina in the distance, sitting on the ground, nursing Cory, surrounded by green lettuces, and headed straight for them. He was on the incident in under a minute.

'It's OK,' said Mabel, who was standing nearby, prodding at the dead snake on the ground, 'it was only a carpet python.'

Andrew looked down at the decapitated creature. Mabel had removed its head from its body with the aid of a shovel.

'It's harmless,' she reassured him.

Andrew looked at Georgina, who nodded as she rocked Cory back and forth. His relief was tempered by the stricken glaze in Cory's eyes and the very real possibility that the snake could have been poisonous. Deadly even. What would he have done then? How could he have lived with himself, knowing he'd failed Cory? Failed Ariel?

'Did you hear that, mate?' he said, sinking to the

ground opposite his nephew, his knees almost touching Georgina's. 'It's harmless.'

Cory looked really scared. He turned wide blue eyes on Andrew. 'Am I going to die, Uncle Andy? Like Mummy?'

'Of course not, mate,' he said, injecting some lightness into his tone, his heart hammering madly in his chest. 'It's going to be OK. Didn't you hear Mabel? It's not poisonous—isn't that right, Mabel?' Andrew asked.

Mabel nodded. 'Absolutely,' she said cheerily. 'That's what I've been telling him. I've lived in the bush for ever, I know my snakes. Been bitten by carpet pythons aplenty.'

Andrew had absolute faith in Mabel's confidence. 'See, you're going to be just fine, I promise, mate.' Andrew smiled. Cory was sitting sideways in Georgina's lap, his cheek to her chest. Andrew's heart melted. He wanted to haul Cory into his embrace and wrap him up safely in his arms. But he looked so fragile at the moment that he didn't want to spook him and he knew that Cory felt secure with Georgina.

Andrew cleared his throat. 'Cory?'

His nephew turned and looked at him. 'I miss Mummy, Uncle Andy,' he said, and crawled off Georgina's lap straight into Andrew's, his skinny little arms wrapping themselves tight like sticky tentacles around Andrew's neck. His little shoulders were shaking as he broke down and sobbed.

Andrew was stunned for a moment. This was it, this was the moment he'd been waiting for. Cory had finally initiated physical contact. Andrew felt his own eyes moisten with tears as he wrapped his arms around his nephew and stared at Georgina, stunned. 'I miss her too, mate.'

Georgina smiled at the man she loved, despite the emptiness of her own arms. He was so obviously moved by his nephew's display of affection and trust. She could see the shimmer of tears in his blue eyes and felt like crying herself.

A man who cried out here was often scoffed at as being less than manly, but Georgina had never seen anything more masculine in her life. She gave Andrew's arm a quick squeeze and roused herself. They were a family of two and she was too involved with them already.

Andrew felt Georgina withdraw and placed a stilling hand on her arm. He knew he wouldn't have got to this stage with Cory if it hadn't been for her. They were going to be all right. He and Cory were going to be OK. It was the first time he'd felt it since his sister's death and he had Georgina to thank for it. Georgina, who he loved.

Georgina, who he wanted to share this moment with.

He put his arm around her shoulders and was grateful when she accepted his embrace. He pulled her in close, huddling the three of them together. No matter what happened after today, at this moment the three of them were as connected as humanly possible.

And it felt so right.

CHAPTER ELEVEN

THE remaining week was hard but Andrew made every last minute count. Much to his surprise, Cory had recovered quickly from the snakebite episode, much quicker than himself, and Andrew had been encouraged by this as further evidence of his nephew's recovering state.

Things fell back into their usual pattern and Andrew revelled in that. Soon enough he'd be back in the city, looking down the barrel of a career in private practice, but he wasn't there yet. He committed the outback scenery to memory. He threw himself with gusto into the work. Every giggle from a shy toddler, every gasp of awe from an elder who could see again he filed away.

They saw three different batches of patients in the last week so they were busy, busy, busy and the time flew by quickly. Interestingly, one of their previous patients dropped in for a follow-up examination. Bobby had been back at Tulla for a week when Jim made a special side trip to bring the lad to Byron.

Andrew couldn't believe how lucky the aspiring cricketer had been. He hadn't ruptured his globe. He hadn't even fractured anything. He did have a severe hyphaema but most of the blood had resolved by the time Andrew looked at it and his vision was remarkably good. He would probably always have some deficit and was going to need close follow-up over the next couple of years. The eye service would see to that and Andrew felt a nagging disappointment that he wouldn't be the one doing it. Continuity was one of the things he was going to miss about being there.

But it was just as well he was leaving. Being near Georgina, loving her and knowing that it wouldn't work, was torture. But being here with her at Byron among her family and her work colleagues, he realised what he'd asked of her that day by the river. How unfair he'd been. She belonged out here. These people were her commitment. Her community. Her family.

He understood that better than he ever had now that he'd made the final breakthrough with Cory. Cory was his family and if you loved someone, you didn't ask them to give that up.

* * *

And then the week was over and it was time to pack up and return to Sydney. Mabel, with the help of the boys, had cooked an enormous farewell feast.

'You didn't have to do this,' he protested, as the table groaned with the most delicious-smelling food.

'Nonsense,' Mabel said dismissively, and winked at Cory. 'Can't send one of my favourite boys off without a party, can I, now?' And Cory beamed.

Andrew took a quick mental snapshot of the scene. The prof and Mabel. Charlie and Cory. Jim and Megan. John and Edmund. And Georgina. All sitting around, laughing and joking and eating. He could feel the portal closing. The brief bubble in time was about to break off and float away and he didn't want to forget this, not ever.

Andrew ushered two tired and loudly protesting little boys to bed as everyone else retired to the front verandah for port and cheese. It took a while to settle the boys as they both bombarded him with the same questions they'd bombarded him with every night the last week. How come they had to leave?

Andrew would have thought that Cory would have been totally put off an outback life after his run-in with the snake. But once the initial shock of being bitten had worn off he'd taken it in his stride. In fact, he had turned it into art—snake paintings were now his favourite subject.

The air was cool when Andrew finally made it back out, only to find that every one else had retired for the night except Georgina. A slight breeze rustled through the trees and wafted a bushy eucalyptus smell their way. It was a full moon, the yard bathed in a milky glow.

She offered him a drink and he took it from her. He could think of nothing better on his last night than spending it with the woman he loved, no matter how bitter-sweet it was.

'They asleep?' she asked, lounging against the railing.

'Finally.' He grimaced. He sipped at his port, the fiery liquid sliding smoothly down his throat. 'Cory's upset. He doesn't want to go.'

'I know,' she said. 'Charlie doesn't want him to go either.' She sipped her own drink. 'So make him happy. Stay.'

Andrew shut his eyes and sighed. 'I can't. Cory might not like it but I'm doing this for him. Ariel trusted me to do what was best for Cory. He's had a great time out here and, if nothing else, working out here has shown me how under-serviced the bush is. Please, try and understand, Georgina. I want Cory to have the best of everything. For goodness' sake, you can't even talk on a phone out here on a cloudy day. And if I'm going to provide him with the best then I need a job that pays well, and as much as I have loved working with the Outback Eye Service, I want to be more financially secure than that.'

'You're wrong,' she said, gripping the railing and blinking the tears from her eyes. He was trying so hard to do right by his nephew he was forgetting the most important thing. 'Stop thinking about what's best for Cory financially or materially. Don't worry about which grammar school you're going to send him to and what political party he'll join. He's an eight-year-old boy—think about what he needs in here...' she tapped Andrew's chest '...to make him happy. All he really needs is you. None of that other stuff matters as long as he's got you.'

For now maybe, but what about later, when he's a teenager? 'It's dangerous out here, Georgina,' he said. 'What if that snake had been poisonous the other day?' The thought had brought him out in a cold sweat ever since.

'It wasn't,' she said calmly.

'Don't be obtuse.' His frustration at their no-win situation boiled over.

She sighed heavily. 'You think living in Sydney is going to protect him from every single thing that can befall him? There are as many dangers in the city as there are out here. They're just different.'

'Of course, but an ambulance is ten minutes away and there's a choice of excellent hospitals. Out here…' he shook his head '…medical help is sporadic at best.'

Georgina felt desperation well inside her. 'All I know is that Cory came here five weeks ago a very different little boy. If you think for a minute that Byron didn't have something to do with his transformation, you're wrong.'

'I know it did, Georgina. I know it was Byron and Mabel and Charlie. And you, more than anything. You helped me reach him and I will be eternally grateful. But we have to get on with our lives. I have a job, an important one. In the city.'

Georgina nodded and swallowed a lump of emotion threatening to choke her. The city. Passed over once again for the city. 'One that bores you senseless. Tell me, Andrew, what do you think would be more important to Ariel? You continuing to chase a thirty-year-old dream that's lost its shine or doing whatever it takes to make her son happy?'

'Cory, of course, but, as you say, as long as he's with me, he'll be fine. And this way I get to do both.'

Georgina shut her eyes. She was all talked out. He had all the answers.

Goodbyes were hard the next morning. Andrew and Cory were catching a ride with Darren, one of the jackeroos who was off to Darwin to see his girlfriend.

'Prof, thank you,' Andrew said, holding out his hand. 'I have learnt so much. I'll never forget it.'

'No. Thank you. You really stepped up to the plate for me, Andy. Are you sure we can't tempt you to stay?'

Andrew looked at Georgina, standing next to the prof. *Easily. So easily.* 'I'm sorry, Harry. I have to do this.'

Edmund and John shook his hand but didn't say anything. They were men of few words and he could sense their reserve. He knew their loyalty lay with Georgina.

Mabel gave him a small basket. 'Something to keep you fellas fed and watered for the long trip.' Darwin was a six-hour drive. And then she opened her arms and swept Cory into them for a lingering embrace.

Charlie and Cory shook hands like two proper cowboys and Charlie gave Cory a parting gift of a black Akubra hat.

'I'm gonna miss ya,' Charlie said. 'Email me.'

Cory placed the hat on his head and smiled.

Georgina was the last one and her heart was so heavy she could hardly bear it. If they lingered too long over this she would crack into a thousand pieces. But whatever she did, it was imperative she didn't cry. Right or wrong, Andrew felt he was doing what had to be done. She knew it was hard for him. She didn't want a fit of hysterical female tears making it any more difficult for him.

He'd made his decision like a man and, damn it all, she wouldn't try and sway him at the last minute. So he had to see that she would be OK. She had to make it easy for him to leave and do what he had to do. Didn't they say that if you loved something you had to set it free?

He pulled her close and dropped a kiss on her head. She pulled back a little and looked into his blue eyes. His scar taunted her as much as it had on the day he'd first arrived. She ran her finger over it.

She cleared her throat. 'Take care,' she said, her voice devoid of emotion.

He nodded. She was so beautiful and he wanted to stay so badly, but she was back to being the Georgina who didn't need anyone. The one he'd seen six weeks ago. It may have been a brave front but it certainly made it a little easier for him to walk away.

She stood on tiptoe and gave him a swift, brief peck on the cheek. 'You're keeping Darren waiting,' she said.

He got the message. *Go. I'll be fine. I'm the can-do girl.* So he coaxed Cory away, who was clinging to Mabel, and they climbed in the car and they drove away.

Georgina felt a little piece of heart go with him. She would not cry. They'd made their bed, they'd fallen in love, despite it not being the smartest thing they'd ever done, and now it was time to pay the piper. And as much as her heart ached now, she wouldn't have given up these last six weeks for all the cattle on Byron.

Two weeks later Andrew could stand it no longer. He missed her. He missed her laugh and her bouncy curls and her rock music. He missed her perfume and her honey eyes. And the traffic in the city was getting on his nerves. And the claustrophobic loom of the skyscrapers gave him the creeps and the coldness of all that glass and concrete made it feel so chilly. He missed the bush. He missed the earthy smell and the wide open spaces. The perfect blueness of the endless sky. The perfect blackness of the star-sprinkled night.

And he hated his job. He hated the predictability. He hated the nine to five-ness of it. He hated how patients were just eyes and not people with family and friends and fears. He was bored and miserable. Would he still be doing it if Ariel had been alive? Would Ariel have wanted him to be this unhappy?

And Cory was sulking big time. He should have rejoiced in that. Six weeks ago his nephew hadn't possessed that kind of manipulative streak, he'd been too grief-stricken, too internalised to play games. But Cory's guilt trip was more than Andrew could stand when he missed Byron and the prof and the eye service...and Georgina, just as much.

But mostly he just missed Georgina. The framed picture of Georgina that Cory had painted hung on the lounge-room wall and he sat each night with Cory, pretending to watch TV when in reality he couldn't take his eyes off the painting. She looked down at him, smiling that zany smile, and he would have given anything to have her step out the frame and be standing in his lounge room.

It was the last straw when Cory burst into tears at the dinner table that night.

'I hate Sydney,' he sobbed. 'I miss George. And Charlie and Mabel.'

Andrew hugged his nephew to his chest as his

little body shook with tears. He missed her, too. He looked at her portrait and remembered her asking him what was more important—a thirty-year-old dream or Cory's happiness? And he had told her as long as they were together, Cory would be all right. But his nephew wasn't all right and he wasn't either.

But luckily he knew how to put it right.

After he'd put Cory to bed, he picked up the phone and rang Byron. Mabel answered.

'Hi, Mabel, it's Andrew. Is Georgina home, by any chance?'

'Andrew, how nice to hear from you.'

He heard the genuine warmth in the housekeeper's voice and wished he was there, eating one of her meals, Georgina smiling at him across the table.

'I'm afraid she's out with the prof. She won't be back for another week.'

He felt his heart sink. Of course, it wasn't going to be made easy for him. Well, it didn't matter if he had to travel to the moon—he had to see her. 'I'll be there tomorrow.'

'Will Cory be coming with you?'

'Absolutely. Just try keeping him away.'

Mabel cackled. 'Will it be a short stay?' she fished.

'I hope not, Mabel. I hope not.'

'I'll get Darren to meet you at the strip. He can drop Cory here then drive you out to George.'

He replaced the phone, a big smile on his face. For the first time in two years things felt right.

Darren pulled up in a cloud of dust at a community that Andrew hadn't visited during his stint with the Outback Eye Service. The jackeroo drove like Bomber flew, and he was relieved to have made it one piece.

It was late afternoon, the clinic over for the day. Little faces peered at him curiously as he greeted Jim and Megan.

'She's with the prof—that way,' Jim said, smiling broadly.

Andrew felt his heart pick up its tempo as he walked along a bushy path. He was acutely aware of his body. The rough sound of his breathing, the clutch of a hand around his gut, the stir in his loins. The sensory input from his surroundings intensified as his anticipation grew. He could hear the almost electric hum of insects and a mournful birdcall. He could smell earth and eucalyptus as he crushed gum leaves underfoot. He felt the air temperature drop slightly as the bush thickened and a cool breeze caressed his fingertips. Leaves rustled overhead.

He rounded a bend and he could see a billabong ahead. He heard the sounds of children laughing and splashing. Georgina was close. He could smell the faint trace of her perfume and her muffled laughter floated towards him on the breeze. His heartbeat picked up another notch.

He entered the clearing and spotted the prof reclined against a treetrunk, his hat over his face. Then his eyes homed in on their target. She was piggy-backing a little girl to the other side of the water. She was splashing some other children as she swam. Their shrieks of laughter died quickly when they spotted Andrew. In fact, the whole billabong fell silent.

Georgina stopped when she realised that the kids had stopped squealing. Something was obviously going on behind her, judging by their curious stares. She felt the hair at the back of her neck prickle as some strange kind of sixth sense warned her of his presence.

'Hello, Georgina,' Andrew said. *Oh, God. She was so beautiful.*

'Andrew,' she said, turning and forgetting to tread water temporarily, nearly drowning her charge. *Oh, God. I look a wreck.*

'Andy!' The prof rose to his feet and hobbled towards him, extending his hand. 'You back for good?' he asked.

Andrew held Georgina's gaze. 'I hope so,' he said. He broke their eye contact and shook the prof's hand, the grip firm despite his slow progress and the old man's obvious tiredness.

'Jolly good show,' the prof said. 'Do you want a job?'

Andrew laughed, Georgina firmly in his peripheral vision. 'Yes, please. I just chucked the old one in.'

'Good, you can have mine.'

Andrew could see Georgina hadn't moved a muscle. 'I would be honoured, sir,' he said. 'As long as Georgina will have me.'

The prof turned and looked at Georgina and winked affectionately. 'She'd be a fool if she didn't,' he said. 'Come on, you scamps,' he bellowed to the giggling, curious children. 'Can't fish with all the noise you're making. Leave Georgie girl alone.'

The prof led the band of wet children back to camp and Andrew watched as they trooped out, the last little girl waving at him, her smile reflected in her big brown eyes.

Finally he and Georgina were alone. He turned back to face her. She was still in the water, staring at him. 'I'm back,' he said.

Yes, indeed he was. He was wearing faded denim and a polo shirt and his blond wavy hair was so familiar and his scar stood out against the stubble on his jaw. God, she'd missed that scar. And he was back.

'So it seems,' she said, finally finding her voice.

'Can we talk?' he asked, holding out her towel.

She shook her head. She wasn't ready to walk out of the water yet, like some scene from a James Bond movie. He was looking at her intently and she felt naked despite her very sensible black one-piece.

'Why are you here?'

'Because I love you and I'm miserable without you.'

Oh, God. 'I'm not living in the city,' she warned.

'I'm not asking you to.'

Georgina swallowed. 'What about Cory? What about your retinopathy cause?'

He shrugged. 'You said it yourself. Above all else, Ariel would want Cory to be happy. And he's been miserable in Sydney. We both have. And I realised I can't live my life being something someone else wants me to be. First and foremost I want to be an eye doctor, and the eye service gave me back my love of ophthalmology. I think Ariel would be happy I've finally found my niche.'

'What about the snakes, the dangers? What about the lack of medical services and technology and schooling? What about giving Cory the best of everything?'

Andrew smiled and shrugged. 'A crazy red-haired sheila taught me that all Cory really needs is me.

She said as long as we're together, he'll be OK. And she was right. I'll cross the other bridges as I get to them. I'm hoping you'll cross them with me.'

Georgina digested the information, her heart pounding. 'What if I told you it was too late? That I can't risk my heart again?'

He wanted to kiss her so badly. Touch her. 'Given what I put you through, I'd say fair enough. But I'm not leaving. I'm still taking over from the prof.' He grinned. 'Are you getting out or am I coming in?'

She couldn't believe what she was hearing. She shook her head. 'I'm afraid I'm dreaming and if I actually get out, you'll disappear like a mirage.'

He chuckled. 'OK, then, I'm coming in.'

He pulled his shirt off over his head, pulled his shoes off and then his jeans. She had the briefest glimpse of his hard, beautifully sculpted body before he dived smoothly into the water. She watched him come towards her in the nearly transparent water. He emerged beside her and hauled her against him. 'Tell me you love me,' he demanded.

Georgina stroked her fingers over his scar. 'You know I do.'

'I want to hear it.'

'I love you,' she said.

He swooped his head down and claimed her mouth in a deeply passionate kiss. Her lips were moist and cool from the water but her mouth was hot inside as his tongue sought hers. He pulled away, knowing he wouldn't be able to stop if he kept going.

'It's more than that,' she said, tracing his lips with her finger. 'I don't just love you. I need you.' Would he understand? 'You're the first man who I didn't have to…be everything to. You didn't need me to organise you or…or spoon-feed you, and you're the first man who took some of the load off me. Hell…' she gave a half-laugh '…I didn't even realise it was a load until you came along and shared it with me. You're the first man I didn't have to…prop up. You let me lean on you. It was nice for a change.'

She thought about the day when the prof had fallen ill and when Bobby had been injured and when Cory had been bitten by the snake. She wished he'd been around when Jen had died, when her mother had been ill, when her body had rejected the new life growing inside her. She could have done with him to lean on then. Just someone to shore her up so she could have kept being brave for her father and John.

He kissed her softly. He could see how hard it

was for her to admit that she couldn't always do it by herself. 'Hey, I'm a man. We like to be needed. You can lean on me for ever.'

'Are you sure? Are you sure you're going to be happy out here? Away from the glitz and the glamour of the city?'

'Wherever you are is where I want to be.' He kissed her nose, revelling in the feel of her curves against his body.

'Really? I'm serious, Andrew. I want you to be really certain. Are you sure you want to give up on your dream of giving Cory the best of everything?'

'This *is* the best of everything. It just took two weeks away from it to realize it. And Cory doesn't want any of that stuff anyway. It's a great life out here, which he adores. As do I. Almost as much as I adore you, and I loved working with the Outback Eye Service and I want to continue the prof's legacy.'

Georgina's heart swelled with pride. Another worry he'd taken off her shoulders—the prof could finally go fishing. 'Well, we can go and visit for a few days every now and then, if you like. I'm not totally culturally ignorant. I like a spot of shopping as much as the next girl. Once or twice a year.'

Andrew chuckled. He hated shopping, too. He hugged her to him, happier than he'd ever been. 'You are going to marry me, aren't you?'

'Absolutely.' She smiled. 'How could I deny Mabel a wedding at Byron?'

He chuckled and lowered his head to seal it with a kiss. And then neither of them spoke for a very long time.

EPILOGUE

THE string quartet played the Wedding March and the crowd beneath the elegant white marquee erected in the front yard of Byron Downs homestead rose to their feet and fell silent. A nervous groom turned around to catch a glimpse of his bride.

There was a collective 'ooh' from the crowd as Charlie and Cory appeared in little white three-piece suits. They each held a little white basket with a red ribbon on the handle. They marched like little robots down the aisle, right foot forward then their left foot level, right foot forward, left foot level—just as they'd practised. They threw out handfuls of rose petals onto the strip of red carpet as they went, their brows furrowed in concentration, each wanting to do their jobs perfectly.

Then another 'ooh' came from the crowd as Georgina appeared. Andrew smiled at her and felt his heart flutter, knowing they would soon be bound together for ever. Officially, anyway.

Unofficially, they'd been bound together since their magical night under the stars here at Byron.

Her dress was a rich creamy satin, the cleavage low, the bodice embroidered with colourful crystals that reminded Andrew of the outback stars. The waist was cinched in and the skirt was full. She didn't wear a veil, her copper curls uncovered. Her red gerbera and wattle-leaf bouquet was a vibrant splash of colour. She looked utterly gorgeous.

Georgina saw Andrew waiting for her at the altar and wanted to hike up her skirt and run to him. Her father, sensing her haste, smiled down at her and held firmly onto her arm, slowing their trip down the aisle, knowing that every bride deserved a grand entrance.

Andrew looked dashing in his black tux, the darkness emphasising the whiteness of his scar, and she just wanted to be down there, marrying him. And suddenly she was there and her father was putting her hand in Andrew's and she didn't want this moment to end. She was with the man that she loved and soon they would be husband and wife.

The celebrant performed the ceremony and there was hardly a dry eye in the house as two hundred guests witnessed Andrew recite 'She Walks in Beauty' as part of his vows.

As Andrew kissed his bride the guests broke out in spontaneous applause and somewhere at the back a wolf whistle shrilled loudly. Cory and Charlie moved forward and the newlyweds swept their boys into a big family hug.

After the dinner the dancing started. Georgina had chosen 'Lean on Me' as their wedding waltz to kick off the festivities. She looked into her new husband's eyes as she swayed to the music and smiled. She had finally found the man she could love and lean on for ever.

Even if he was a city boy.

MEDICAL™

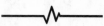

Large Print

Titles for the next six months...

January

SINGLE DAD, OUTBACK WIFE	Amy Andrews
A WEDDING IN THE VILLAGE	Abigail Gordon
IN HIS ANGEL'S ARMS	Lynne Marshall
THE FRENCH DOCTOR'S MIDWIFE BRIDE	Fiona Lowe
A FATHER FOR HER SON	Rebecca Lang
THE SURGEON'S MARRIAGE PROPOSAL	Molly Evans

February

THE ITALIAN GP'S BRIDE	Kate Hardy
THE CONSULTANT'S ITALIAN KNIGHT	Maggie Kingsley
HER MAN OF HONOUR	Melanie Milburne
ONE SPECIAL NIGHT...	Margaret McDonagh
THE DOCTOR'S PREGNANCY SECRET	Leah Martyn
BRIDE FOR A SINGLE DAD	Laura Iding

March

THE SINGLE DAD'S MARRIAGE WISH	Carol Marinelli
THE PLAYBOY DOCTOR'S PROPOSAL	Alison Roberts
THE CONSULTANT'S SURPRISE CHILD	Joanna Neil
DR FERRERO'S BABY SECRET	Jennifer Taylor
THEIR VERY SPECIAL CHILD	Dianne Drake
THE SURGEON'S RUNAWAY BRIDE	Olivia Gates

™ MILLS & BOON®

Pure reading pleasure

1207 LP 2P P1 Medica

MEDICAL™

─╴√╴── *Large Print* ──╴√╴──

April

THE ITALIAN COUNT'S BABY	Amy Andrews
THE NURSE HE'S BEEN WAITING FOR	Meredith Webber
HIS LONG-AWAITED BRIDE	Jessica Matthews
A WOMAN TO BELONG TO	Fiona Lowe
WEDDING AT PELICAN BEACH	Emily Forbes
DR CAMPBELL'S SECRET SON	Anne Fraser

May

THE MAGIC OF CHRISTMAS	Sarah Morgan
THEIR LOST-AND-FOUND FAMILY	Marion Lennox
CHRISTMAS BRIDE-TO-BE	Alison Roberts
HIS CHRISTMAS PROPOSAL	Lucy Clark
BABY: FOUND AT CHRISTMAS	Laura Iding
THE DOCTOR'S PREGNANCY BOMBSHELL	Janice Lynn

June

CHRISTMAS EVE BABY	Caroline Anderson
LONG-LOST SON: BRAND-NEW FAMILY	Lilian Darcy
THEIR LITTLE CHRISTMAS MIRACLE	Jennifer Taylor
TWINS FOR A CHRISTMAS BRIDE	Josie Metcalfe
THE DOCTOR'S VERY SPECIAL CHRISTMAS	Kate Hardy
A PREGNANT NURSE'S CHRISTMAS WISH	Meredith Webber

MILLS & BOON®
Pure reading pleasure

1207 LP 2P P2 Medical